Caster & Fleet

THE
CASE
OF THE
DECEASED
CLERK

PAULA HARMON
LIZ HEDGECOCK

Copyright © Paula Harmon and Liz Hedgecock, 2018

All rights reserved. Apart from any use permitted under UK copyright law, no part of this publication may be reproduced, stored in a retrieval system, or transmitted, in any form or by any means, electronic, mechanical, photocopying, recording or otherwise, without the prior written permission of the copyright owners.

This is a work of fiction. Names, characters, businesses, places, events and incidents are either the products of the author's imagination or used in a fictitious manner. Any resemblance to actual persons, living or dead, or actual events is purely coincidental.

ISBN-13: 978-1719926157

For Miss M C Smith

Lady Superintendent at the

General Post Office

who was said to 'never turn an opportunity

for women down'

Liz Hedgecock

CHAPTER 1
Katherine

'Shocking shenanigans,' muttered Ada under her breath, but even in the gloom of the music hall auditorium I could tell she was suppressing a grin.

James leaned close. 'It's a shame I didn't think to bring her to the Merrymakers last summer,' he whispered. 'She'd have sorted the situation out in half the time.'

'She'd have sorted me out first.'

'And so she should have. You painted woman, you.' He kissed my ear. My giggle brought a glare from Ada.

'Madam,' she said to Aunt Alice, 'would you like me to sit between Miss Kitty and Mr James? They're misbehaving.'

Aunt Alice gave a half-hearted tut. A few weeks ago, after a year's genteel courtship, she had left our home to walk down the aisle with Mr Frampton, a stalwart of the cycling club. Aunt Alice had relaxed in the warmth of marital ecstasy and I'd finally been able to explain precisely what Connie and I had been doing last summer, and why. We'd brought her to the Merrymakers to help set the scene. A matinee had seemed the safest performance, as the level of sobriety in the audience and the inoffensiveness of the acts was likely to be higher.

I leant across and whispered, 'Aunt Alice, I do hope you're not finding this too alarming.'

Aunt Alice waggled her head. Clearly she wasn't going to make any judgments just yet. She was holding her husband's hand under the table as if she wasn't sure it was allowed. On the other side of Aunt Alice were Albert and Connie. Two married couples, Ada, James and I...

'And now for Ellen Howe and a brand-new song!' Mr Templeton bellowed from the stage.

The orchestra struck up, and with a sinking heart I recognised the tune.

'Oh dear,' I said. 'I didn't know they were going to play this at the matinee.'

'What?' asked James.

Ellen, her sleek brown hair piled on her head, came on stage in a loose shapeless dress and began to sing:

> *'I went out courting the other night*
> *And I must have looked a terrible sight.*
> *My waist was gorn,*
> *My bust was flat,*
> *I was roughly the shape*
> *Of a bowler 'at.*

How could I forget?
I was feeling such a fool —
I never forgets my corset, see,
Not as a general rule.
I thought...
Oh dear, where 'as my corset gorn?
I feel almost as bare as the day that I was born.
I've petticoats, chemises
And bloomers if you pleases,
But I forgot my blessed corset,
I left it down in Dorset.
Oh dear, I really do feel bare.
It's just as well my best boy doesn't seem to care!'

'Oh my!' gasped Aunt Alice. 'How shocking. Can you imagine?'

Her husband muttered into her hair and she giggled. It was rather disturbing. They were both getting on for fifty years old.

'What sort of trollop would go out without her corset?' murmured Ada on one side of me. I glanced sideways at her. She was still looking at the stage but that suppressed grin was back.

'I can't imagine who wrote this song,' whispered James into my other ear.

'Shh,' I said. I looked at Connie. She raised a glass and winked.

***

'So, do you think we've given your aunt a taste for the music hall?' said Albert over supper. Despite the fact that they had finally stopped honeymooning several months ago, he was kissing Connie between courses, to the utter horror of other diners nearby. It was just as well we had a corner table.

'I doubt it,' I said, crumbling my roll. 'Aunt Alice is definitely more forgiving of what she would call "vague improprieties", but she's still quite proper. When she moved out she left strict instructions to Margaret to chaperone any visits by James. Of course, Margaret only chaperones when she wants to be annoying. Unfortunately, that's most of the time.'

I looked at James, but he was studying his plate. Normally I loved it when the four of us went out together, but this evening I wasn't hungry. Something seemed to have come over James all of a sudden. His previous good humour had vanished, and he appeared anxious. We hadn't had five minutes on our own so that I could ask. He too was picking at his food and the waiter was collecting half-full plates.

'Have you heard Reg's news?' asked Connie.

I nodded. 'Yes, he came to see me after work on Wednesday,' I said. 'I mean, after he finished work. I was at home.'

'Oh yes,' said Albert, 'I'd forgotten Dr Farquhar had gone on sabbatical. What will you...'

He blushed. He and Connie were clearly still concerned that I might be worrying about money. They must have realised that the loss of Aunt Alice's tiny private income into the household finances would cause difficulties, and now they knew about the additional loss of Dr Farquhar's salary.

'It's only for a few months, while he goes on his lecture tour,' I said. 'He has given me a financial retainer and the good news is that I don't have to keep typing his name. I was forever getting it wrong.'

'That's good,' said Connie, smiling.

'Going back to Reg…' James prompted.

'Oh yes,' said Connie. 'He's been promoted. Someone in the Department spotted his potential and gave him an opportunity to train as an office boy. Before we know it, he'll be a clerk. He's over the moon. His prospects are wonderful. We gave him some smarter clothes. Maria wanted to refuse, but we said it was a reward for all his help.'

No-one, not even James, knew that on Tuesday I had an appointment with Mr Maynard, one of the most senior men in the Department. I had no idea why he'd invited me and suspected that as an office boy, Reg would be earning the same as me if I returned to the typing room. That was the way of things. Yet something about Mr Maynard's letter had suggested that I would not be a typist again. While the income would come in very handy, the truth was that I was intrigued to discover what he had in mind.

'Anyway,' said Albert, 'Connie and I have things to do. I mean we're having an early night. I mean…'

It was quite baffling that after nine months of marriage they still blushed.

'Be off with you both,' said James, 'I'll see Katherine home safely.'

His smile didn't reach his eyes. I knew he felt the same as me, that he wished they'd leave us and go home. I felt ashamed. Connie was my best friend.

'I'll settle the bill as we leave,' said Albert. 'My treat.'

James and I were alone. We were silent. The waiter bustled and cleared the table. We ordered coffee. We were still silent. Normally it didn't matter. We could spend hours with each other chatting or arguing or saying nothing, reading or daydreaming or taking in the view as we cycled. It was simply enough to be together for the short periods people would let us be alone with each other. Well, not enough, but it was all we seemed to have. What was equally unusual was the seriousness on James's face; how he looked away when our eyes met; the way he fiddled with his coffee cup. Not for the first time, I wondered if his love had all been a dream and I was about to wake up.

After what felt like a year, I spoke. 'What is it, James? You know you can tell me anything, no matter how awful.'

James sat back in his chair and looked at me. His hand reached out to touch the little curls on my neck which had escaped the hairpins. The expression in his eyes was anxious. He leant forward and held my hand.

'Katherine,' he said, 'will you —'

A strange voice said 'I thought it was you.'

We both jumped. A very attractive woman was standing next to us. Medium height and dressed in the latest fashion, she gazed down her nose at me with such mocking disdain that I wanted not only to recoil but also check to see if I had spilt something or my hair had come down.

'Geraldine,' said James, dropping my hand. 'What are you doing here?'

'Mrs Timpson, if you please,' said the woman. 'As you recall, I requested that any former intimacy between us should cease.' She turned to me. 'I gather you are his latest — well, I wonder what you are? Lady-friend, conquest, paramour…' I felt my face burn. 'I can see you're neither wife nor fiancée. Unless he can't afford a ring, but that's unlikely. Perhaps he's no longer so impetuous.'

'Leave her alone,' said James in a low, cold voice. 'Leave her alone, Geraldine. She is worth a million of you.'

'As I said, Mr King, you should address me more formally. A word to the wise, Miss.' She leaned down so that her face was level with mine. 'You would have to be *insane* to continue an entanglement with this man.' She straightened up and walked to a table on the other side of the room.

I swallowed. My hands shook. James took them in his but he was trembling too.

'Katherine,' he said, 'please believe me, that woman is poisonous. It's not…'

I willed my voice to be steady. I withdrew my hands and gathered my things. 'We agreed to always be honest with each other.'

'Yes, we did,' said James, holding my arm to stop me

rising. 'I just . . . I never wanted to have to think about her again. But she's part of the reason why —'

'Why what?'

He paused, looking at me. 'I want to ask you something,' he said. 'I've wanted to for a long time, but it might explain why I've waited so long.'

'I don't understand.' I stood up, and I felt my legs shaking.

James rose and offered his arm. I stood and took it. I could sense Geraldine Timpson watching us.

'Will you come and visit my family?' said James.

It was the last thing I'd expected him to say. I walked out of that restaurant with all the dignity I possessed, wondering if I'd ever want to go there again; if I wanted to go anywhere with James ever again. He hailed a cab, my arm still locked in his other elbow. Without making a scene, it would be hard to get away.

'Who is that woman?' I asked.

'Will you come and visit my family?' he repeated. 'We can go tomorrow and come back on Monday evening.'

'I have things to do on Monday.'

'Can't they wait?'

'It depends on whether you explain about Geraldine. Sorry, *Mrs Timpson*.'

'That's why I want you to come home with me. I mean, to my family home.'

'Why now?' In the open air, my shock and embarrassment hardened into anger. 'You've never once offered to introduce me to them in the eighteen months we've known each other. Not once. Why now? I know you're ashamed of having to introduce a woman who has to earn her own living, but —'

'What? No, Katherine, you're completely wrong. It's nothing like that. It's the other way round.' He handed me into the cab and followed to sit beside me.

'I don't understand,' I repeated. 'How can you be ashamed of your family? You have a nice house in the country, don't you? They're respectable, aren't they? You know my family. We are all slightly mad. How can yours be any worse?'

He tensed.

'What?' I asked. 'What have I said?'

In silence, he leant forward with his head in his hands. 'This isn't how I wanted today to end,' he whispered at last.

My anger drained. I dropped my bag and put my arms around him.

'No secrets,' I said. 'We promised.'

Chapter 2
Connie

'Do you think…?'

'I try to,' said Albert, smiling. 'Do I think what?'

'If you'd let me finish, you'd know by now.' I sighed and looked out of the carriage window at the mixture of dark shadows and blazing lights that was evening London. I leaned closer before I continued, not because I was afraid of being overheard — we were alone in the carriage, and Tredwell was on the box — but because it seemed secret, and not my secret. 'Do you think they'll get married?'

Albert put an arm around me. 'K and James, you mean?' He pursed his mouth, considering. 'I imagine so. I hope so.'

'Yes,' I said eagerly. 'They're just right for each other.'

'You mean they're equally impulsive and, occasionally, downright eccentric.'

'Exactly, a perfect match.' I paused. 'I'm a bit worried about Katherine,' I continued.

I felt Albert's hand closing round mine. 'In what way?' he murmured.

I sighed. 'A money way.'

'Mm,' he said. 'Me too. I doubt Dr Farquhar's retainer will keep the good ship Demeray afloat. But you know K is too proud to say so. It's how to help without making it completely obvious.' He squeezed my hand. 'I've made sure Margaret's expenses at Oxford will be picked up from the start of term.'

'Through your father?'

'Nominally, yes. He committed to pay for Margaret's education, so K can't quibble over that.'

'You're so clever,' I said, kissing him.

'Why, thank you. And you're so complimentary,' he said, returning the kiss.

'Maybe Katherine could find another job until Dr Farquhar returns,' I said, sitting back and fanning myself. Despite the March chill outside, the interior of the carriage was growing distinctly warm.

'Yes, perhaps.' He grinned. 'A double act with Ellen at the Merrymakers? Although I wouldn't want you out till all hours on singing duty.'

'Oh don't.' I smacked him lightly on the arm. 'My days of stardom have ended. I don't think Katherine would ever want to do it again.' A thought popped into my head. 'Wait... Now that Aunt Alice has moved out, perhaps Katherine could find another lodger. It would be company for her and Miss Robson, too. In fact — maybe

Miss Robson might know someone suitable.'

'It's a thought,' mused Albert.

'I wish she and James would just get married,' I confided. 'They bicker as if they are, already.'

Albert grinned. 'I can't decide if they'd be a steadying influence on each other, or go even further astray.'

'I think you know the answer to that,' I countered, as we drew up outside the house.

***

On our return from honeymoon we had taken a house in Marylebone. After much debate we had settled on a neighbourhood that was smart and convenient for town, and also not too close to either of our families. It wasn't that we wanted to hide, exactly; more that we wanted to be private.

Mother, of course, had had plenty to say as she swept round the rooms on her first visit, wrinkling her nose at the wallpaper and the curtains. 'Well, so long as you're happy,' she said, running a finger along the mantelpiece and examining it. 'It isn't how I'd want to live. So *narrow*.'

'It's a lovely cosy house,' I said defensively. 'If after a while we don't like it, we can always move. We're only renting.'

Mother sniffed. 'I just hope that you don't have to go any lower.' She walked to the window and gazed at the street.

'We have four floors and an attic,' I snapped. 'That's plenty of space for two people and servants.'

'Ah yes, servants.' Mother looked pointedly at the mantelpiece, and her mouth curled at one corner. 'If you need any advice on managing them, Constance, do let me know.'

Albert had borne my ravings calmly when he had returned home. 'Connie, your mother's favourite hobby is provoking you. Just rise above it,' he said, taking my hands and kissing me.

'Don't try and divert me,' I said, backing away. 'The worst thing is when she's rude about you. She said Father was carrying you. If she only knew, oooh —'

Albert advanced and put his forefinger on my lips. 'She doesn't know, Connie, and your father and I would like it to stay that way. The business will be back on its feet soon.' The finger stroked my chin.

'I suppose,' I said. 'It makes me want to lease a mansion in Chelsea, though.'

Albert frowned. 'Don't you like it here?' he asked.

'Yes, of course I do,' I said quickly. 'It's just — so different being married, and having a house and servants of my own.'

I hated to admit it, but I was beginning to see what my mother had meant on all those occasions when she had sniped that the household kept her busy. She had flatly refused to let me take Mary with me. 'Your servants are your responsibility, Constance. I have recruited my staff over several years, and I am not allowing you to poach them.' So I had read up in Mrs Beeton, placed advertisements in the *Times*, and interviewed a host of lady's maids, housemaids, and cook-housekeepers, before settling on the applicants who seemed most cheerful and least frightening. Albert had brought Tredwell with him, and Tredwell had procured a butler and footman from his acquaintance. They were hard-working, efficient, and reliable. My staff were pleasant, forgetful, and already leaving dust on the mantelpiece, but I feared that if I took them to task about it I would end up with something worse.

'Oh, Connie.' Albert gathered me in his arms. 'You look so down in the mouth.'

I felt my lip wobbling, and buried my head in Albert's shoulder so that he wouldn't see. 'I thought we'd go out together and have fun,' I said. 'I didn't think about the house, and furnishings, and the menus, and — and everything.'

Albert stroked my hair. 'I didn't think I'd be spending so much time on work,' he said. 'It's much harder to rescue things than it is to start from scratch. Especially when you're dealing with someone who's convinced he knows best.' His voice lowered to a growl. '"You may be riding high now, Bertie, but over time we'll see who comes out ahead."' The imitation of his father was accurate enough to make my shoulders stiffen.

I looked up at him. 'You're in charge of his affairs, though, aren't you?'

Albert nodded. 'He likes to go up to the bank and issue orders to Anstruther. Buy this, sell that, here's the way to go. I've told Anstruther to make polite noises and do nothing without my agreement.'

'Good.' A sudden thought struck me. 'My father's not…?'

Albert laughed. 'In comparison, your father is a pleasure to deal with. He just had a run of bad luck. It could happen to anyone.'

'I suppose,' I said. 'It won't happen to us, though, will it?'

'Not if I can help it,' said Albert.

***

Despite the fun of the Merrymakers, and a good dinner, I lay awake for a long time, listening to Albert's regular breathing beside me. How was it that he had what felt like the financial affairs of the world on his shoulders, and yet was sleeping like a baby, while I had nothing to worry about except getting a decent meal out of our servants, and I was a bundle of fret and worry?

You're being ridiculous, Connie, I told myself, turning over as gently as I could. *Think of all the things that have happened; all the expeditions where none of us knew if we'd come back safe.*

Albert flung a heavy arm across me and mumbled something about jute.

You just need something to distract you. Or Mother. Jemima's baby was due in the following month, and I had great hopes that Mother would become a doting, ever-present grandmother, and be too busy to harry me.

Then again, what would happen when we —

The thought grew till it filled the room and made it hard to breathe. I couldn't manage three servants properly — what on earth would I do with a baby? I wasn't even sure that I liked babies. We would need a nursemaid, and a nanny, and in time a governess, and I would have to recruit them all.

I wriggled out from under Albert's arm. 'Whassit?' he murmured, stirring.

'Nothing,' I whispered. 'Just a — a bad dream. I need a glass of water.'

My hand shook a little as I poured from the carafe. I took the glass to the window and peeped round the thick curtains. The street was relatively quiet now, with the occasional carriage going past. Everyone in the neighbourhood was probably asleep. I had made calls, and left cards, and received visits, and I was confident that no-one of my relatively limited acquaintance in the area would be singing bawdy songs in the wings of a stage, or pursuing another cab through the night, or chasing a dream of black tulips —

I remembered Albert's words about Katherine and James earlier that evening, and my response. If they did marry, they would probably set out on more escapades than ever, as a joint enterprise.

And Katherine wouldn't need me any more.

Oh, for heaven's sake. I rubbed my eyes with the sleeve of my nightgown, drained my glass, and set it on the nightstand. We would still be friends, of course we would. I got back into bed and wriggled into the warm spot I had occupied before.

Albert's arm slid over the counterpane. 'Do you feel better?' he asked.

'Yes, thank you.' He grunted, and the regular

breathing resumed.

Outside a carriage passed at speed. Who was inside, and where were they going?

And a little voice whispered to me: *You need an adventure.*

Chapter 3
Katherine

James lifted his head and tried to smile, but it was no good.

'Please tell me who Geraldine is,' I said. 'Or should I call her Mrs Timpson?'

'You can call her anything you like, I'm sure you've learnt suitably foul language by now.'

'James, please.'

The wheels of the cab clattered on the road, and snatches of voices, horses, other wheels came in through the window.

'A friend at Oxford invited me home,' he said at last. 'He had a sister, Geraldine. She was by far the loveliest girl I'd ever seen — or at least I thought so at the wise old age of nineteen. She was seventeen and seemed so demure, hanging on my every word as if I were the wisest, most erudite being in the universe.'

'Seemed?'

'Yes. None of it was real. Her whole purpose in life was to marry a rich young man. And there I was, rich enough, young and terribly flattered. I was too naive to see through the artifice, so I proposed.'

I gasped. 'You were so concerned about Henry — even though he and I never had a proper "understanding" — and yet you didn't tell me you'd been engaged yourself?'

He reached for my hand. 'I know, I'm sorry. I've always tried to forget it. I suppose I was afraid.'

'You?' It seemed impossible. James's work involved mixing with slum dwellers and ruffians. I didn't think he was afraid of anything.

'Who broke off the engagement?' I asked, bewildered.

'No-one. Geraldine simply married someone else when I was studying at a German university. On my return I went to her family home demanding answers, and her father said she had been too young to make any binding promises. He handed me a note in which she severed all connection with me and in particular, with my family.'

It was hard to know what to say. The cab had pulled up outside my house. The horse clopped its hooves and the cabbie made soft croonings to it.

'That's why I wondered about Henry,' James said, his thumb rubbing the back of my hand. 'I wanted to know if you were the sort of woman who would disregard a promise when someone else came along. It was unforgivable of me. You are not the same species as

Geraldine.'

'I see,' I said, eventually.

'The thing is, her decision wasn't about *me*,' he said through narrowed lips. 'I would have "done". I was a rich young man with good connections. That was all she cared about. Timpson is no better, or worse. The issue was what she discovered about my family. I was devastated at first, then I put it behind me. I realised I'd never really been in love with Geraldine, nor she with me. After that I decided most women weren't worth sixpence and threw myself into my work, until one strange evening in Hendon when a small redhead kicked me in the shins. Since then I've been afraid to say how I feel, in case you don't feel the same. I can't risk losing you.'

'Perhaps you should take the risk,' I said. 'I shall be ready to visit your parents tomorrow.'

***

There was so little time to prepare for a weekend in the country. I toyed with the idea of wiring Connie, but decided not to bother her. The chances were that she was chuckling with Albert about matters domestic or romantic. Doubtless there would be a baby soon, and we would drift apart. It would be nice to be godmother, but Connie had three sisters. Even if I were, I had no idea how to hold a baby and would probably drop it in the font.

Instead of sending a telegram I posted Connie a letter, asking if we could lunch on Tuesday at the restaurant where we'd first met. I couldn't bring myself to write about Geraldine, but somehow I needed to tell Connie how anxious I felt.

James is taking me to Berkshire to meet his family. Please don't read anything into this. He seems worried about it and I don't know why. Oh Connie, maybe soon I'll be trapped in that awful typing room again with nothing to stretch my mind. Oh well, maybe I'll make a funny old maiden aunt for your children and grandchildren and tell them about our adventures, and they won't believe that we ever did anything so exciting. Please excuse me. I promise to cheer up by Tuesday.

***

Grimy old London slipped away in no time and the countryside appeared in a thousand shades of green. The Thames and its tributaries rolled gentle and leisured, almost clear. I had to restrain myself from pointing things out to James as if he were four, but fortunately a small girl got into the carriage with her mother at the first stop and I entertained her instead. Perhaps being a mad 'aunt' to Connie's children might not be so bad, provided all I had to do was exclaim when I saw a herd of cows, or a mother duck and her ducklings.

James sat next to me dozing. There were shadows under his eyes as if he'd been awake all night. We were on the slow stopping train and after a while, I tired of the view and simply ached from the jolting train. I let James's head slide onto my shoulder, and held his hand. He didn't stir until we arrived at Courtney Abbas, his tiny home station.

'Nice to have you home, Mr King,' said a porter as he opened the door. 'Standish is waiting with the trap. Is this your young lady? Let me help you down, Miss. Don't worry about the smuts. Grubby old things, trains, but you'll soon be at Hazelgrove and able to freshen up.'

We stepped out of the station into a country lane and James handed me into a trap. The driver turned and touched his cap.

'Nice to meet you, Miss Demeray. I'm sorry I couldn't bring the carriage for you, and I hope you're not offended, but the axle's damaged. And it is a fine day.'

'Yes, it is,' I said. The air, particularly after the fug of the train, was sweet. Birds sang overhead and whirled in the blue sky. Courtney Abbas village was like a painting, and the road to James's home was winding, pretty and pot-holey. I could see why an axle might have been damaged.

James sat opposite me and leaned forward. 'Are you all right?'

I nodded, but now that he was awake I saw the tension in his face, and my hands clenched inside my gloves.

We arrived at a tall pair of iron gates, beyond which was a large house. It was not as grand as the Swift or Lamont houses but it was easily three times the size of mine, and the garden was immense — by London standards, at any rate.

'Can you let us down here, Standish, and take our things round?' said James. 'We'll walk the rest of the way. I feel as if my legs have gone to sleep. Are both Father and Mother at home?'

'Yes sir, and Miss King is up and about today.'

'That's good to hear,' said James, lifting me down to the path.

'Indeed, sir.' Standish clicked at the horse. We stood and watched the trap rattle away.

'Here we are,' said James.

'It's lovely.'

'Yes, I suppose it is.' He paused, then took my hand and led me towards the house. It seemed so serene. I could imagine his family taking tea on the lawn, being so very calm and polite. I hoped James's fire and energy were not hereditary, or it would be an exhausting weekend. As we neared the front steps, he took a deep breath. The door opened and a manservant ushered us in. A small maid took my cloak, and another led me into the drawing room. This was Connie's world, not mine.

***

James's parents were charming. His mother was dressed in black silk and sat by the fire with her embroidery, looking much as I remembered my own mother, in a similar style of dress. I needn't have worried that my clothes weren't up to the minute. Her smile was warm and welcoming, as if we were old friends.

'I am so pleased James has finally brought you to see us, my dear.'

I looked sideways at James. He stood silent and didn't catch my eye.

'I gather you're Roderick Demeray's daughter,' said Mr King. 'I very much enjoyed his books. It must be difficult waiting for news, but I hear that you're a practical young woman. Very — capable.'

'Very modern,' his mother added, with not so much approval as hope. She patted the seat next to her and I sat down. 'We keep a quiet house,' she continued. 'I think it's rather too dull for James, but hope that one day he'll want to settle here.' She had a wistful air. 'Do tell me about your work. James told us that you worked for a government office. Edwin knew someone in a government office. I wonder if it's the same one.'

'Andrew Fowler was a fool,' said Mr King. 'But then, most government men are fools. I daresay you think so too, Miss Demeray. You were a typist, weren't you? I expect you had to copy a lot of drivel set to send an honest taxpayer to an early grave.'

'I like to think that you're the managing sort,' said Mrs King, as if her husband hadn't spoken. 'And modern. You must be very brave. I do like a woman who can cope with anything.'

It was a strange conversation. James was fidgeting by the mantelpiece. The grandeur of the house was so at odds with the man I knew, who met me one day in a fancy restaurant and on another in a café frequented by junior clerks; who dressed as a working-class man to learn the truth about the urban poor; who was happier to sit on a river bank with a bun and a bottle of beer than to sit in Simpson's.

'Father, would you mind if I showed Katherine the

house?' James still looked ill-at-ease. 'Where is Evangeline? I hear she's been up and about today.'

His parents exchanged a glance, and each peeped at me before looking away.

'I sent her to lie down until luncheon,' said Mrs King. 'She is very keen to meet Miss Demeray, but we can't have her over-excited.'

'I'd love to see the house when I have changed,' I said. This was true; but I also wanted time alone to think.

'Here's the key to the library,' said Mr King. 'I'm sure Miss Demeray would like to see it, when she's ready. Her father's books are in there.'

James escorted me from the drawing room and we stood at the bottom of the stairs while the manservant summoned a maid.

'Why does he keep the library locked?' I asked.

'To keep my sister out.'

I stared at him. Whatever did they think she'd do?

'Father thinks novels are racy, and a bad influence on her.'

I felt my face flush. I had been reading novels since I was eleven. And here was his sister, who must be at least thirty years old, more protected than fine china. Did they think *I* was racy?

'Your parents seem very strict with her,' I said. 'It's no wonder you don't find it frustrating visiting me. Aunt Alice's fussing is nothing, compared to not letting me out at all.'

'You know perfectly well I find it frustrating. But

you're right, it's not the same.' He was still tense. 'I don't think Evangeline's left the house or garden for ten years. It's not her fault.'

A demure young maid appeared.

'Good morning, Miss. I'm Norah, and I'll look after you. Let me show you your room. I've put out nice hot water for you and shaken out your dresses. And I'll take your travelling clothes and brush them for you.'

***

In a pretty bedroom, finally alone, I stood at the washstand. With scented soap I washed away the smuts and grime from the train journey, and wondered if I had enough time to brush my hair and put it back up. There was a knock at the door. Surely James wouldn't —

I put on my wrap, tying it tightly round me, opened the door a fraction, and peered round it. A woman stood there, and there could be no doubt who it was. She had the same dark hair and hazel eyes as James, the same twinkle.

'I'm Evangeline, James's sister. May I come in?'

'Um, yes, of course.'

Evangeline was, like her mother, dressed in black at least ten years out of style, but she was as pretty as James was handsome. She studied the dress I was about to change into, which Norah had unpacked and laid out on the bed. 'Is that the latest style?'

'It's last year's. I mean the style, not the dress. The dress is older, I've had it remodelled.' I realised I was gabbling and stopped. Evangeline looked fit and healthy, though pale. She was bright-eyed, and seemed intelligent. It was hard to imagine why she was made to rest, barred from the library and apparently imprisoned within the grounds.

'Could you show me how to do my hair like that, for dinner?' She had picked up the magazine from my open suitcase, and was studying the cover.

'Of course, if you'd like.'

'I do admire you,' she continued, her eyes shining. 'You have such adventures! James's letters about you are wonderful — the ones he sends me, anyway. The ones he sends Father and Mother are very dull. He sends mine through Norah, so Father won't know. Father would never let me read about your adventures. He'd think them overstimulating.'

I could feel my cheeks burning. What on earth had James written about me?

'He loves you so much,' said Evangeline. 'It just pours through his words.' She smiled. 'I'm sorry, I've made you blush. I've really come to tell you about myself.'

'I'm sorry, I don't understand —'

'I don't suppose he knows how to explain,' she continued, 'so I think I ought to. There was once a woman who broke his heart, and it was because of me. It took him years to get over it. So if you're going to do the same, it's probably best to do it straight away. The doctors say I'm mad, Miss Demeray. James doesn't think so. But everyone else does. Even Father and Mother believe it may be true. The horrid woman he was engaged to simply married someone else without a word. They're afraid of the tainted blood, you see.' Evangeline looked straight into my eyes. 'Are you?'

CHAPTER 4
Connie

'What are your plans today, Connie?' Albert wiped his mouth with a napkin and dropped it on the table. He began to push his chair back, but caught my eye and stopped.

'I shall do errands this morning, and go to the library,' I said, wishing I could make it sound more important. 'I'm having lunch with Katherine, and after that we'll see.'

'That's good,' said Albert. 'I was thinking of lunching at the club. If you'd been at home I could have come back, but —'

'It's quite all right,' I said, rising. 'I can amuse myself, you know.'

Albert raised an eyebrow, then got up. 'In that case, I shall see you later.' The footman opened the door for him, and I heard his quick steps ascending the stairs. I kept my eyes down as I left the morning room. I did not want to see the expression on the footman's face, or think about what he might tell his colleagues later, in the servants' hall.

I stood in the hallway for over a minute, pondering where to go. I did not wish to follow Albert upstairs like a sheep. I opened the door to the parlour, but Nancy was dusting. In the end I sat in the cold, empty dining room, at the bare table, trying and failing to think, until I decided that meeting Albert on the stairs was preferable to another moment in that chilly place.

I reached my boudoir without further encounters, sank into the armchair, and stared at the fire. It wasn't Albert's fault I was bored.

We had gone for a lovely drive in the country on Sunday afternoon, making the most of the warm spring sunshine. It had felt like the first days of our marriage. But on our return a note had been waiting for Albert, addressed in his father's familiar crabbed hand, and he had disappeared into the study, emerging an hour later with a bulging envelope and a frown. 'Take this round, Johnson,' he said, handing the envelope to the footman, 'and be quick about it.'

'Is everything all right?' I asked, once Johnson had departed.

'Of course,' he snapped, then ran a hand through his hair, and sighed. 'I'm sorry, Connie, that wasn't fair. Father was questioning my judgement on a particular matter, without good reason. I, um, felt the need to argue my case.'

I reached up and smoothed Albert's hair back into

place, then stood on tiptoe to kiss him. 'Well, it's done now. Let's enjoy our evening.' Yet despite a mostly well-cooked dinner, and a glass or two of claret, Albert was subdued, and had spent most of the time after the meal buried behind the newspaper.

I longed to hear about Katherine's visit to James's family. What were James's parents like? Was he different at home? Had he — had he proposed? I felt sure that Katherine's worries about the weekend were unfounded, and her vision of herself as a maiden aunt to my — our children was preposterous. If we had any she would be a wonderful aunt, but I was sure not a maiden one. What else had she said? There had been more, but in my excitement over James I had skipped through the rest of the letter. 'I'm just going to look for something,' I said to the newspaper, which grunted.

The letter was tucked into the left-hand pigeonhole of my bureau; the one I kept for unanswered correspondence. I scanned the careless, slanted writing, so characteristic of Katherine. Where was it?

'...*soon I'll be trapped in that awful typing room again...*'

Was that what Katherine was planning to do while Dr Farquhar was touring the country, telling amusing stories about his life in medical practice? A return to Miss Charles and eight-hour days pounding the typewriter, and no free time? That must be why she had asked me to have lunch at the grim, drab little restaurant where we had first met. She would be working nearby, again.

Oh, Katherine.

That was why she had said Tuesday, not Monday; because she would be asking for her old job back the moment she returned from the countryside.

I put the letter into the pigeonhole and closed my eyes, recalling my first encounter with Katherine. She had been reading the letter which had brought us together, eating something unappetising, and as prickly as a thistle. Or — no — as prickly as the hard casing of a horse chestnut. Her frown, her briskness, her hunched shoulders would all return. I blinked away a tear.

We had to help her. But I knew better than to approach Albert in his current mood of financial grumpiness, particularly when it had been caused by his sense of familial duty. I closed the bureau, picked up my novel, and rang for Violet to take down my hair.

***

In my eagerness I arrived at the restaurant fifteen minutes before the appointed time, and nursed a cup of tea until Katherine's short, slight form appeared in the doorway. 'I'm sorry I'm a bit late,' she said, sliding into the seat opposite. I tried to read her expression, but couldn't.

'How are things?' I asked. It seemed the safest opening.

Katherine reached for the menu, but didn't read it. 'Odd,' she said.

I pushed my tea aside and took her hand. 'Tell me.'

Katherine's mouth twitched. 'Where do you want me to start, Connie?'

'The beginning?'

She rolled her eyes.

'All right, tell me why you're late. Ten minutes late, in fact. My tea's lukewarm, and I'm hungry.'

'You're always hungry.'

'Oh, do get on with it, Katherine. We can bicker another time.'

'What can I get you ladies?' asked the waitress, who seemed to have come out of nowhere.

'I'll have the beef pie, please.' While Mrs Jones meant well, her pies always drooped in the middle and the filling was soggy. I had never realised how good our — Mother's — cook was until I left. 'My treat, Katherine.'

A smile flitted across her face. 'Can I have poached eggs on toast, please? And a pot of tea.'

'Right you are,' said the waitress, whisking away.

'Trust you not to take advantage of a square meal,' I grumbled.

'It's very kind, but you don't have to. I'm not a charity case.' Was the prickliness coming back? I could have left then and there but curiosity, and of course hunger, kept me seated.

'So,' I prompted. 'Your lateness.'

'Oh yes.' The smile broadened. 'I had an appointment with Mr Maynard at the Department.'

'Mr Maynard?'

Katherine waved her hand as if it was obvious who he was, but her expression was still distant, as if she were trying to solve a puzzle. 'He's one of the Group

Chief Clerks.'

'And . . . are you returning to the typing room?'

'No. Well . . . no. Miss Charles has enough typists at the moment, although she does seem rushed off her feet.'

'Oh.' *Perhaps she'll let me help her so she doesn't have to work.* Then I saw that Katherine was picking at her napkin in the casual way of someone waiting for a prompt. 'Go on.'

'But . . . there was another opening.'

'What sort of opening?' I asked; not that I had any clue of office hierarchy, or, indeed, what people in offices actually did.

'Mr Maynard wants to establish a new section. A kind of research bureau.' I imagined the bureau in my boudoir filled with miniature typists. 'And they're looking for someone to run it.' She paused. 'Mr Maynard had approached Miss Charles and she suggested me. Hence his letter. He grilled me for an hour, then asked me to obtain a reference from Dr Farquhar. So I've been at the telegraph office sending a complicated wire. I hope I caught him before he sets off to Derby or Cambridge or Liverpool or wherever he's going first.'

The waitress set down a pot of tea. 'Your food will be here shortly.'

'Thank you.' I watched Katherine stir and pour. 'Do you know what you'll be doing, exactly?' I asked.

Katherine fiddled with the handle of her teacup and shook her head. 'He said I'd get more details when I started the job. When, not if. No, I don't understand either,' she said to my raised eyebrows.

'Maybe it's secret,' I whispered.

Katherine snorted. 'I doubt it. He's probably just trying to draw me in. But the money's good, and it's only three days a week.'

'That is good news,' I said. 'I'm sure Dr Farquhar will write you a glowing reference.'

'So long as he doesn't mention the music hall, or the time we were drugged in a tearoom —' She broke off as our meals arrived. 'Although something Mr Maynard said made me wonder if he already knew…'

'Perhaps the job will be even more exciting.' It seemed doubtful, but I wasn't sure what else to say about it. I picked up my cutlery. 'How was your weekend?'

'That was odd, too.' Katherine pricked her eggs and watched the yolk ooze out.

'Nice odd?'

'I thought you were hungry,' said Katherine, nodding towards my plate.

'For news, as well,' I said, trying not to sound aggrieved as I sawed at my pie.

'I'm not sure how much I ought to tell you,' she said.

I laid down my fork. 'Katherine, we're friends. If you ask me to keep a secret, I shall. There must be something you can tell me.'

'All right,' she said quietly. 'James's parents live in a lovely house in the country. They welcomed me, and seemed anxious that I had a nice time while I was there.'

'What about James?' I asked, my food forgotten. 'How was he?'

'Attentive. More than he is usually.' Katherine cut a square of toast and egg. 'We went for a walk all together on Saturday afternoon, and on Sunday, and went to church with James's father.' She glanced up at me, and that casual invitation was there again.

'Didn't James's mother accompany you to church?'

'She did not.' Katherine had the look of someone who wasn't sure whether to proceed. Then she shrugged. 'She stayed at home with James's sister.'

'I didn't know James had a sister. Is she older or younger than him? Was she nice?'

'She seemed very nice. Well, as much as I saw of her.' Suddenly Katherine put her head in her hands. 'Oh, this is ins — No, ridiculous,' she said firmly. 'It's ridiculous.'

I gawped at her. 'I don't understand.'

Katherine laughed, a sudden, mirthless laugh. 'Neither do I.' She leaned forward, and her voice was low and urgent. 'James's sister hasn't left the grounds of their house for ten years. She's dressed in the style of ten years ago, just like her mother. They lock the library in case she reads something she shouldn't, even though she's older than you or I. And when I met her, she told me that everyone but James thinks she's mad.'

CHAPTER 5
Katherine

'Come in,' said Miss Robson when I knocked on her door early on Wednesday morning.

I entered. I had rarely been into Miss Robson's bedroom in the five years she had lodged with us. She dusted it herself and Ada did the rest.

Miss Robson didn't turn immediately from her seat at the desk and it struck me how slender and young she appeared from behind, her brown hair not yet greying and as neat as Margaret's, with just a gentle wave.

'How can I help you, my dear?' It looked as if she had been reading old letters. They were strewn across the desk, thin at the creases. The ribbon which had tied them was faded a little where the knots had been. A photograph of a pleasant-faced man, neat-featured, his hair greying at the temples, stood on the corner of her desk. 'Did you and Mrs Lamont have a lovely lunch yesterday?'

I pulled a face. 'Not exactly. The food is barely edible. It was good to talk with Connie, though.'

Miss Robson started to bundle up the letters. 'I was sorry to miss your return from Berkshire. How was your weekend?'

I fidgeted.

James and I had returned to London early on Monday morning in a train so full it was impossible to sit together, let alone talk. Connie hadn't believed that we'd had no time alone in Hazelgrove, but it was true. His parents had been so thrilled to have a visitor. When I had changed for dinner, Evangeline arrived with Norah to have her hair put up in the latest style. After dinner, when James and I might have met in the moonlit garden, the house had been full of creaks, patterings, and low voices on the landing: 'Back to bed now, Miss, no wandering.' I hadn't known if someone was diverting James's sister or warning me. And finally we'd said polite farewells as I boarded a cab at Paddington, since when I'd heard nothing from him. 'Work will be busy this week,' he'd said, and kissed my cheek.

'His family are charming,' I said. 'Miss Robson, I hope you won't think this is forward, but I do hope you'll trust me. I need to speak with James without interruptions and I've asked him to visit me at six p.m. tomorrow.'

'It's Ada's half-day.'

'Yes.'

She glanced towards the photograph.

'We will behave, I promise.'

Miss Robson gave a sudden laugh. 'Really Katherine, I'm neither your mother nor your aunt. You are a grown woman, capable of making your own decisions. I presume you'd like me to take Margaret somewhere.'

I felt my face grow warm.

'Yes. I hope you don't mind. I've bought three tickets for a performance of *Princess Maleine* and asked Margaret to bring a friend. I wouldn't ask, but…'

Miss Robson patted my arm. 'I consider you my friend, Katherine, and you seem overwrought at the moment. When you feel the need to talk to someone, if Mrs Lamont is not available, please don't hesitate to speak to me. I understand about James and I am never judgmental. I wonder, would you call me by my Christian name? I have lived in your home for so long.'

Tears pricked my eyes. Until she'd said it, I hadn't thought of myself as overwrought. Nor had I thought of the house as anything but 'our' home.

'Of course,' I said. 'Of course I shall.'

'That's wonderful.' She smiled broadly and held out her hand as if we'd only just met. 'Mina. Well, that's the shortening. Much like Mrs Lamont, I'm not fond of the longer version of my name.'

We shook hands.

'And I'd be delighted to take Margaret and her friend to see *Princess Maleine*. As I say,' she touched the photograph, 'I do understand about James and trust you to know your own judgment.'

'Thank you . . . Mina.' I suppressed a giggle. It

seemed very odd.

'And what are your plans for today?' she said, looking at my office outfit.

'I have to speak with someone about a job at the Department. I met with him yesterday and he asked me to return today.'

'Really? That's very quick for the Department. When Andrew worked there he always complained about how long it took for anything to happen.' She gazed at the photograph.

'Oh, I didn't —'

'Andrew had . . . gone before you began work there.' She turned back to me. 'Are you going to type for Miss Charles again? Surely it's not necessary.'

'Oh no, if I'm successful I'll be working for a Mr Maynard.'

Mina frowned. 'Mr Maynard,' she said, more to herself than to me. 'How curious. Anyway, on with you, or you'll be late.'

She was right. I took the underground from Walham Green and was at St James's Park in no time. I wondered how much time I might have saved in the preceding three years if I had ignored Aunt Alice's warnings about tube trains.

The night before I had posted a letter to Connie, asking her to meet me for lunch. I asked her not to bring Albert.

I had also posted Evangeline, or rather Norah, a parcel containing all the back issues of *The Woman's Companion* that I owned.

Now, straightening my hat and smoothing my suit, I entered the Department ready to see what Mr Maynard had to say.

A messenger boy led me down a long dark corridor lined with heavy oak doors, until we reached a spiral staircase lit by immense windows.

'Just two floors up, Miss Demeray,' he said. 'It's the only door. Room 2M. Do you want me to show you?'

'Don't worry, I'll find it.'

Men passed me as I ascended, every single one pausing at the sight of a woman without a mop in the main part of the office.

Voices floated up after they'd passed.

'Maynard's new project. Only wants women.'

'Can't be important then.'

'I expect it'll be more typewriters. Clatter clatter clatter, or do I mean chatter chatter chatter?'

Laughter. Nothing had changed.

I knocked on the door of Room 2M and stepped inside. It was panelled in oak, large and airy. The high ceilings were corniced and moulded. Close to the high windows, three desks were arranged as an incomplete square. A fourth, larger desk was set slightly apart but facing in to them. Each desk had a typewriter on it. They looked a little abandoned but would, on a sunny day, sit in a pool of light. A few empty bookcases, a set of index card drawers and a large filing cupboard were incongruous along one wall. I walked to the window and peered down to the street below, where under grey skies people beetled about. From this height and distance it was impossible to do more than guess at the pedestrians' size, age, or class. I wondered if James was out there, rushing about. What articles he had been assigned to write this week. Whether he would visit at six p.m., or not.

'Good morning, Miss Demeray.'

I jumped. Mr Maynard had emerged from behind one of the panels. He was a tall, imposing man with the broad shoulders of a sportsman and yet he moved as stealthily as a cat. His thick hair was white and his brown eyes twinkled.

'Good morning, sir.'

'Congratulations. You have the job.'

I was startled. As Miss Robson — *Mina* had said, nothing ever moved quickly as a rule. I opened my mouth to say thank you, but Mr Maynard waved a hand and continued. 'Welcome to your new office. This is your desk.' He pointed at the larger one. 'I imagine you want to know what this is about.'

'Yes, sir.'

He sat at what he had said was my desk, and I sat at one of the others. He steepled his fingers, contemplating me. I wondered when the other women would arrive, and what they would be like. I had never been in charge of anyone before, unless you counted Ada. But only a fool would try to make Ada do anything she didn't want to. Connie, Albert and certainly James would say I was bossy, but it wasn't the same as running a section.

'I think it will rain later,' said Mr Maynard.

I glanced outside. 'Yes, sir.'

'Right. Down to business. I've heard good things about you, Miss Demeray. Miss Charles was very disappointed when you resigned, which manifested itself in her complaining that you became "giddy" towards the end of your earlier time with us. After some digging I established that you had returned late from your lunch break once, and had taken a few days' leave at short notice. Otherwise she said your work was exemplary and in fact you had, and I quote, "improved the English of several reports she had been asked to type".'

I grimaced. I didn't think anyone had noticed.

'Don't worry. Only Miss Charles spotted it. The originators probably congratulated themselves on their succinctness of phrase.'

Mr Maynard stood up and withdrew a key from his breast pocket.

'This team however, despite all evidence to the contrary, will not be copy-typing. Any typing you do will be of your own reports. And yes, I am aware that you have been engaged in, um . . . shall we say . . . *adventures*.' He hummed a tune and my mouth dropped as I recognised it. 'I do like an evening at the music hall. It makes a great deal more sense than government, and it is far more amusing. Oh, and Dr Farquhar also mentioned the matter of the black tulips. *Most* interesting.'

Mr Maynard unlocked the cupboard and retrieved a box of papers, which he put in front of me. I was puzzled. There were magazines, handbills and articles, from which earnest men and women peered, beckoning.

I flicked through them, and frowned.

Mr Maynard sat down and steepled his hands again.

'As you know, the Civil Service has no real place for women at present unless they're typing. As a brother of four sisters and a father of three daughters, not to mention as the husband of a very intelligent wife, I think this is absurd. My hands are tied officially, of course, but there are places only women can go and conversations only women can have, and that is where you come in. My *argument* for setting up this section was to ensure these individuals were not evading tax with clever accounting. You would like my paper. It is well-written. My *purpose,* however, is different. You will wish to pick your own team. I imagine you may have at least one lady in mind already. Just as an aside, no-one need know anyone's marital status if that's a consideration. Now, as to what the real aim is…'

***

'I can't work in an office,' said Connie. Her knife and fork were suspended above her veal and ham pie. It never ceased to amaze me how she could eat a full meal at lunch time and not fall asleep in the afternoon.

'Of course you can. Thousands of men infinitely stupider than you do it every day.'

'I would have no idea what to do. I haven't sat at a desk since I was fourteen.'

'It's not like that, anyway,' I said. 'Well it is, sort of, but I can explain. I need a team, and I need you. Mr Maynard wants you anyway — he couldn't have made it any clearer. Besides, it's mainly investigation work and you're fully trained in that.'

'Albert would never let me.'

I took a deep breath, and then a mouthful of poached plaice, and watched various expressions cross Connie's face. Worry, fear, doubt, excitement.

'Connie,' I said, 'I'm not blind or stupid. I know you love Albert more than anything, but there's something wrong. Can I make a guess that part of it is that deciding on menus every day is not as much fun as wondering what escapade I'll drag you into next?'

She sighed, laid down her cutlery and put her head in her hands. 'Oh Katherine, I'm so bored. And the servants are so horrid, apart from Tredwell. I don't know what to do with myself every day. I can't tell you how much I look forward to meeting you for lunch. All right. Tell me what it's about.'

'It's about fraud.'

'I was very bad at arithmetic.'

'No, listen. We don't have to calculate anything except our own expenses. I'm sure you can manage that. But you know about the craze for mesmerists, mediums, astrology and all that sort of thing?'

'Harmless parlour games, surely.'

'Sometimes. And then there are the times when it isn't, and people are hurt or taken advantage of. Mr Maynard wants a small group to investigate behind the scenes, under the pretext of ensuring sufficient tax is being paid on income. In reality he wants more than that. Exposure of fraud, and exploitation. And the perception is that women are drawn to it more than men.

We have a chance of finding out things that perhaps men can't.'

'Albert won't like it.'

I bit my lip. *No more secrets.*

'I'm sure you can find a way to talk him round. Just try it for a bit, Connie, and let's see what we can dig up. It's only parlour games, as you say. There can't be too much risk.'

***

James arrived at five past six. He was surprised when it was I rather than Ada who let him in and took his hat. I led him into the drawing room where he kissed me on the cheek and sat by the fire. His shoulders were damp with rain, and I started to brush it off before I could stop myself.

'Hullo,' he said.

'Hullo,' I replied.

'I'm sorry. I've been very busy and forgotten to ask about the job. Were you successful?'

'Bother the job.'

'Pardon?' James looked startled.

'I said "bother the job." I want to tell you something. I need to get this straight because I can't bear it any more.'

He frowned. 'Shouldn't we go out if you want to talk privately? Any moment now Margaret will bounce in.'

'No she won't. We have the house to ourselves. And before you ask, bother the neighbours too.'

'Katherine, I —'

'Hear me out.' I stood, caught sight of myself in the

mirror over the fireplace, wished I hadn't as my hair was coming down at the back, and sat next to him.

'James, I just want to make this clear and then hopefully we'll both know where we stand. Please listen to me. I'm hurt you didn't tell me about Geraldine. I'm annoyed that you've been entertaining your family with tales about me when I thought you hadn't told them anything. But I don't care what may or may not be wrong with Evangeline. It makes no difference. I would like you to explain it, but ultimately it has nothing to do with how I feel about you.'

'Which is?'

'Exactly the same as I did on Saturday night before that woman turned up. If you don't go back to your usual rude self soon, I'll kick you in the shins so hard you'll be able to display them as novelties.'

He dropped his hands and grimaced, but there was a grin behind it. 'Better not risk that,' he said.

'No. And to be quite clear, your parents may think I'm modern, someone in the office thinks I'm an adventuress and right now I'm alone with a man, but I'm not so modern that I'm going to say things first which *you* ought to say first.'

There was silence. But it was the normal silence. James pulled a face as if trying to work out a particularly difficult sum, then leant forward, took a strand of my hair and began to curl it round his finger. Our faces were very close.

'I love you, Katherine. I love you.'

'Good, because I love you too.'

He chuckled. I thought he would kiss me but instead, he sat back and dug in his jacket pocket. He dropped a glove in my lap.

'Oh,' I said, 'I wondered where that had gone.'

'I stole it,' he said.

'Why?' The glove was rather old and thin, and a little grubby.

'I needed to know what size your finger was.'

He held out a small box and opened it. A ring with rubies and diamonds twinkled up at me. 'I've been carrying this around since Saturday evening,' he said, and leaned forward to kiss me.

The drawing-room door burst open. Ada stood brandishing an umbrella, sodden and dripping. 'Miss Kitty! Mr James!'

Then her glance fell on the ring box.

'About time too,' she snapped, and then grinned. 'Well, Miss Kitty. I'm going back out to send some wires. I'll get Mrs Bertie and your aunt here so we can share the bottle of my sister's elderflower wine I've been saving for when Mr James finally got round to popping the question. So you've got ten minutes alone. You can't do too much damage in ten minutes.' She slammed back out.

James leant forward again. 'I don't want a secret wedding,' he said. 'But by all that's infuriating, I want a quick one.'

CHAPTER 6
Connie

Katherine had had to return to work straight after lunch. 'Why don't you come too, Connie?' she asked me, with a twinkle in her eye. 'You could see the office, perhaps even meet Mr Maynard…'

'I'm not sure that's a good idea,' I replied, putting on my gloves. 'I need to think about this. I don't want to give him the wrong impression.'

Katherine sighed. 'I understand,' she said. 'I don't want to press you, but —'

'Yes you do.' I stood up.

She laughed. 'All right, maybe I do. But please, Connie, give me an answer soon.'

I wandered the shopping streets of London for some time, though if anyone had asked me about the window displays, or the new fashions, I would not have been able to give a coherent answer. I remembered my wakeful night, my longing to do something exciting, something *more*... But I had never so much as entered an office. I could not type. I had no shorthand. I wasn't even sure that I could set out a business letter. I imagined the other women looking at me pityingly, and Katherine growing exasperated that I couldn't even pretend convincingly. My cover as an office worker would probably be blown on my first day, and I would be sent home in disgrace. I stopped, and caught sight of my reflection in a shop window. Her shoulders sagged, and her hand gripped her bag as if she expected someone to steal it. She looked defeated before she had begun. I shook my head at her, and trudged away.

***

To pass the time, and perhaps also to try and redeem myself as a human being, I decided to call on Jemima. I had to wait on the doorstep for some time before I was admitted, and was shown to Jemima's bedroom. She was propped up in a nest of pillows, wearing a frilly bed-jacket. Her hair cascaded over her shoulders. A half-completed game of patience occupied a tray which, in turn, rested on her rounded stomach.

'I'm actually glad to see you,' she said. 'Apart from Mother, and the doctor, and Charles of course, I've seen no-one but servants for weeks. I feel as if I'm in quarantine.' Jemima's laugh was almost a cackle. 'Perhaps pregnancy is contagious.' The tray wobbled dangerously. 'Move that, would you, and ring for Jane.'

Within seconds I heard running feet. 'Is everything all right, ma'am?' gasped Jane.

'Yes, Jane. I am as well as I was five minutes ago

when you showed Connie in. Can you bring afternoon tea. Connie will need plenty, she's very hungry.'

'Yes, ma'am,' said Jane. 'What would you like? I could bring up a milk pudding, or some gruel and water toast —'

'Not gruel,' Jemima snapped. 'If I never saw gruel again in my entire life, it would still be too soon.'

'I am sorry, ma'am,' Jane said, raising anxious eyes to her mistress's face, 'the doctor did say to be careful, and you know how worried the master is about you —'

'Just toast, please,' said Jemima, with a heavy sigh.

'How is your new doctor?' I asked, when Jane had curtsied her way out of the room.

'Young and scared. Do sit down, Connie, you're making the room look even more untidy.' Jemima glared at me until I complied. 'I don't know where Dr Farquhar found him — at a prep school, perhaps. Farquhar himself ought to be shot. Deserting me in my hour of need…' Jemima's gaze drifted to the window. 'What is it like outside?'

'It's fresh and breezy, but not cold. The crocuses are out in the park. Would you like me to open the window?'

Jemima cast her eyes to the ceiling. 'Good Lord, no. Charles is petrified that the least draught will carry me off. All the servants sneak to him. No getting out of bed,' she thundered. 'No rich food, it's bad for the baby. No wine. No novels, in case I over-excite myself.' Suddenly she thumped the coverlet with her fists. 'I thought I was having a baby, not becoming one.'

'It'll be over soon,' I soothed.

'Yes.' Jemima reclined against her pillows. 'I cannot wait for the day when I hand it to the wet-nurse and emerge into the world once more.' She grinned. 'Like a butterfly coming out of its cocoon.'

A light knock at the door, and Jane entered with tea-things, finger sandwiches, and a selection of cake. 'Here is your toast, ma'am,' she said, putting a plate of thin, dry toast into Jemima's hand. 'I'll pour your tea; we must remember not to make it too strong, mustn't we?'

'Yes, we must,' growled Jemima. 'Thank you so much, Jane.' She waited until the maid's footsteps had died away before continuing. 'I'll have a ham sandwich, a crayfish sandwich, and an egg and cress sandwich to start. And don't you dare eat all the scones.'

I loaded a plate and passed it to her. 'What about your toast?' I asked.

Jemima made a face at it and gave the plate to me. 'You can have it if you like.'

***

Jemima sent me home in her coach. 'There's no point in you taking a cab,' she insisted. 'It isn't as if I'll be going anywhere, is it?'

I thanked her, and kissed her cheek. 'I'll see myself out,' I said.

'Come again soon,' said Jemima. 'I need a square meal.'

When I arrived home Johnson informed me that Albert was expected at half past five. 'He went to the club for lunch, ma'am, and then I think he said he had a meeting.'

Another meeting. 'Thank you, Johnson,' I said, handing him my things and heading for the stairs. 'I shall be in my boudoir.'

Half past five came and went. It was almost six when Albert came home. I thought about staying where I was, and letting him find me; but that seemed churlish. I walked onto the landing. 'Did your meeting over-run?' I asked.

Albert started, and looked up. 'No,' he said, tersely. 'I played a few games of billiards at the club afterwards.' He seemed — not untidy, but disarranged, somehow, and his cheekbones had the high spots of colour which usually only appeared after a few glasses of wine. 'I'll be in the study.'

'Come and talk to me, Albert,' I said. 'I've hardly seen you today.'

Albert frowned. 'We had breakfast together.'

'That was hours ago.' My eyes flicked to Johnson, who was still in the hallway. 'I can tell you about my visit to Jemima.'

A grin wiped the frown away, and I found myself smiling too. 'You visited Jemima? How is she? Good-humoured as ever, I dare say.'

'I think she's finding confinement rather trying,' I said, as he came upstairs.

I took the armchair, and Albert sprawled at my feet as we roasted ourselves in front of the fire. The story of Jemima and her afternoon tea made him laugh, and while I was glad that he seemed happier, I wondered what he would be like in that situation. Would I be confined to bed for three months?

'And how was Katherine?' Albert asked, stroking my ankle. 'Did she get her job back?'

'Not exactly.' His touch tickled, and I reached down to rub my leg. 'She's got a better one.'

'Oh good.' The stroking resumed. 'What will she be doing?'

'She's running a bureau.' Albert shifted round to look up at me, making an impressed face. 'They'll be doing important work.'

'I'm sure they will.'

'She's very excited.'

'K's always excited about something.' Albert's fingers eased the heel of my slipper off.

'I know. She even tried to recruit me,' I said, laughing.

The fingers stopped dead. 'I beg your pardon?'

'Don't worry, I have no intention of taking her up on it.'

'I should think not.' After a pause, he began to caress my foot again. 'As if I'd let you slave over a typewriter all day for a pittance.' He snorted.

'It's not about whether you'd let me,' I said. 'It's about whether I choose to, or not. And I don't think I'd be very good at it.'

'Noooo…' I frowned at the amusement in his voice. 'You could break a nail, or anything.'

'It isn't that sort of work, anyway.'

He shrugged. 'It's work. You don't need to work for a

living. And if I could persuade K to accept help, neither would she.'

I put my slipper back on. 'So if I worked for free, that would be all right?'

Albert twisted round. 'What is this? What are you trying to wriggle round to?'

There was an edge to his voice which I didn't like, but my temper was roused. 'I'm not trying to wriggle round to anything.'

'Good.' Albert got up. 'I don't suppose it occurs to you that if any of our acquaintance saw you going out to work, they would assume it was a matter of necessity.'

'Oh, our acquaintance.' I stood too, to stop him looking down at me. 'You didn't worry about them before we were married.'

'That was different.'

A timid knock at the door made us both jump. 'Come in!' called Albert.

Johnson advanced with a salver, on which lay an envelope. 'Telegram, sir.'

'Thank you,' said Albert, ripping it open. His eyes scanned it, then he passed it to me. 'Sorry, it's for you. I'd read it before I realised.'

I tuned Johnson's stammered apologies out as I read: *Great news Mr James finally asked our Miss Kitty come and celebrate STOP Ada.*

I looked up at Albert, my anger jolted away. 'At last,' I said, and my heart felt as if it would burst with joy.

'Yes.' He smiled. 'Just in time. Hopefully this will put an end to whatever crackpot scheme she's pulling you into. Johnson, tell Tredwell to get the carriage out. We'll go round at once.'

'We?' Warmth crept up my neck. 'The telegram was for me, not you.' I knew it was petty, but I didn't care.

'In case you've forgotten, I'm family.' He rounded on the footman. 'Why are you still here, Johnson? I gave you an order!' The footman, still apologising, bowed himself out of the room in a flash.

'I can't stop you coming,' I said, drawing myself up to my full height. 'But if you persist on behaving like some sort of — *dictator* — then you ought to stay at home. You aren't fit company for anyone at the moment.'

'How dare you,' Albert said, very quietly, and that quiet was far worse than if he had shouted at me. He strode out without another glance.

We sat as far apart in the carriage as we could, gazing out of opposite windows. My anger had not abated one jot; in fact, I was angrier that Albert had spoilt Katherine's news, and might spoil the party. I fumed silently until we drew up outside the house. The drawing room was ablaze with light. It was an occasion indeed.

Ada was looking out for us, and threw the door wide open. 'Come in, come in!' she said, beaming.

Albert turned to me. 'At least someone wants me,' he remarked. 'Shall we?' He offered his arm, and, after a hesitation which I hoped no-one had noticed, I took it.

Katherine and James were sitting together on the settee, holding hands. 'I'm so happy for you!' I exclaimed, embracing Katherine and shaking James's hand.

Katherine regarded me as if I were a puzzle to be solved. 'Come upstairs a moment,' she said. 'I want to show you some fabric Aunt Alice has put by, and of course I can't let James see.' She kissed his hand before relinquishing it.

We didn't speak again till we were safely upstairs in Katherine's bedroom. 'Now, Connie,' she said, taking both my hands, 'what is it? You look all — strained.'

'Are you still going to run the bureau?' I asked.

She nodded, eyes wide.

'We quarrelled,' I said, squeezing her hands. 'I was right about working with you. Albert didn't like it, and he won't let me. But I don't care, after what he said. I'm in.'

CHAPTER 7
Katherine

'So,' I said, 'what do we do next?'

I sat on the edge of the supervisor's desk sipping tea. Pretty much the first thing we'd put in the filing cabinet was a portable stove. No messenger boy would climb two floors of a spiral staircase with a tea tray. We had to drink it black, but it was better than no tea at all.

'We shall discuss your wedding plans,' said Connie. She sat back in her chair, stretched, then leaned forward and typed a three-letter word, scowling at the machine as if daring it to bite her.

The same piece of paper had been in her typewriter for a week. Periodically, she would add to a nonsensical sentence by hitting the keys with one finger in the same way she would have poked a loaded mousetrap. I suspected Connie would never get beyond uneven letters and bruising her finger when it slipped between the keys. She sighed, rose and came over to get a biscuit from the plate next to me.

'Yes,' said Mina, 'or do we have to discuss the meaning of the expression "tea break"?'

I had no managerial control whatsoever. When no-one else was there to listen, which was most of the time, we addressed each other without formality. It still seemed odd to be calling Miss Robson by her first name. Aunt Alice, whose friend she'd been since childhood, rarely called her anything but Miss Robson. But that was Aunt Alice all over. I wondered if she called her husband 'Mr Frampton' even when carried away with emotion. I felt a smirk form at the thought.

'How can you blush and grin at the same time?' said Connie. 'Anyway, wedding.'

'You know perfectly well: wedding in four weeks' time at my St Jude's. It was either that or James's parents' parish, but I wanted to be married by the vicar who christened me, in the church I've attended all my life.'

'I don't know how you can bear to wait.'

'Now who's blushing and grinning? Some of us are patient and unimpetuous.'

Mina laughed and poured herself more tea. 'Two adjectives which, as far as I can gather, have never applied to you, Katherine.'

'So there's nothing more to say about my wedding,' I said. 'Where do we start with Mr Maynard's problem?'

I didn't want to talk over the impending day any further. All the dress fittings and planning made my head ache. Connie would be matron of honour, Margaret would be bridesmaid, but I was still hoping James could persuade his parents to allow Evangeline to attend and perhaps be another bridesmaid. I had sent a piece of the blue silk to Hazelgrove so that Norah could trim an outfit to match the trimmings on the others' dresses, but it seemed a vain hope. And every time I read Mrs Beeton's idea of a wedding breakfast, I almost wanted to cancel the entire thing and join a nunnery. Almost.

'Well, if we can't persuade you,' said Mina, putting down her cup, 'back to work.' She walked to the empty desk and indicated several stacks of paper. 'I've arranged our investigations into the five who seem most likely to be fraudsters.'

'Can we be sure they're all fraudsters?' said Connie.

'I think so. If they're not, then we can prove them to be as genuine as it's possible for these people to be.' Mina spoke with the sort of distaste you'd expect if she'd trodden on something unpleasant. Connie and I exchanged glances.

'I've pulled together the documents we've collated for each of them. Katherine's hours in the library looking through old newspapers and illustrated magazines were invaluable. You must have found it immensely dreary.'

'Not at all,' I said. 'I had to stop myself getting sidetracked, but it was like a treasure hunt once I got into a routine.'

'And Connie's sketches are very interesting. Not to mention the notes she took from her conversations at social gatherings.'

'It made those awful dinner parties, soirées and at-homes infinitely more bearable,' said Connie. 'I actually had something to talk about. I just find it quite astonishing how many people are involved in this sort of thing.' She paused and a soft smile crossed her face. 'I'm glad the sketches were good.'

To no-one's surprise but Connie's, she was the one with the eye for capturing simple but accurate likenesses from memory. Since she really was patient and unimpetuous, she weighed things up and was a better observer.

'And I have consulted what official records Mr Maynard was able to procure for me,' Mina continued. 'I think there may be a link between these five persons. I'm not entirely sure what, or why.'

We perused the piles of paper. The desk was otherwise empty, as so far I hadn't managed to find a fourth member of the team. Connie had been a necessity. I didn't know how she'd talked Albert round, and perhaps didn't want to know, but I couldn't work without her.

Asking Mina to join me had proved fruitful. I knew she would be an asset, a woman of quiet method and stubborn determination. She had been a private secretary her entire working life, and she had contacts with a network of intelligent women intent on gaining the vote. I knew she would be perfect, but if it hadn't been for her employer's partial retirement, she would not have been free to work with me. The money was a consideration of course, since she had no other means of support, but when we were alone after dinner, and I had explained the focus of the research I had been asked to undertake, her usually calm face clouded. She banged her fist on the table. Then she took a breath. 'Yes. I will join your team. Not just for you, but for Andrew.'

Now, a few days later, she had brought all our information together. On the top of each pile was a handbill.

The first was of a man, his hair oiled and smooth as lacquer, his pale eyes staring, his hands reaching out. 'Let Professor Vitruvius read your mind — your most hidden thoughts are no challenge for THE SPHINX.'

The second picture portrayed a simpering girl. She gazed heavenwards with impossibly blue eyes, her hands clasping flowers. Petals were caught in her flowing golden hair. She appeared to be emerging from a cloud of butterflies.

'I wish I looked like that,' said Connie.

'Nonsense,' said Mina. '"AELFRIDA, found in a bluebell hollow, a visitor with messages from Fairyland" is forty if she's a day and wearing a wig. They've painted over the photograph. You ought to know, you made a sketch of her coming out of her house.'

'I know. I don't want to look like the real thing. I want to look like that image.'

'I'm sure Albert would find it perfectly sickening,' I said. But I knew exactly what she meant.

A more traditional portrayal of a magician was third.

'Could be James before he shaved off his moustache,' said Connie. 'I keep meaning to ask, do you miss it? Does it make a lot of difference when he kisses you?'

'Please stay focussed, Mrs Lamont,' I said.

'Blushing again. And Miss Swift while I'm here, if you please.'

'Be quiet.'

'Ladies,' admonished Mina.

The Great Ludolphus was displayed in an amalgam of Indian and Arab dress and wearing a bejewelled turban. In every other respect he looked like an average Anglo-Saxon. His eyes, coloured as blue as Aelfrida's, gazed from the paper as his hands hovered above a sleeping woman suspended in mid-air.

'Is he going to tickle her, molest her, or wait to see if she'll bounce when she hits the floor?' said Connie. Her words mocked but I sensed discomfort beneath. Ludolphus's expression had a menace it was hard to define. He promised to turn age into youth, water into wine, lead into gold.

'The future is known only to BASSALISSA, gypsy queen,' declared the fourth handbill. 'Be THRILLED by her amazing predictions!' A woman, her stance similar to Professor Vitruvius, stared up from a crystal ball. For a change, her eyes had been coloured a deep unlikely green and the hair which curled onto her shoulders was raven-black. She wore a translucent veil held down by a chain of coins.

'Another wig,' said Connie. 'Her hair's naturally ginger. It makes yours look very dull, Katherine.'

'Thank you.'

'I think you should try that veil and coin effect with your wedding dress.'

'Why, what a wonderful idea. It will look lovely with an ivory silk gown and a blue flowered head-dress.'

'Ladies,' repeated Mina. 'Please concentrate. By location, here we have the Clapham Sphinx, the Acton Fairy, the Hammersmith Alchemist, and the Wandsworth Gypsy. I think we should investigate them in turn. We need to discover what they're gaining from their activities. Is it simply entertainment or is something else being promised? Is the audience entertained, or tormented? Those are the questions we must answer. I have some ideas of where to begin, but I do believe, Katherine, that we need a fourth member; perhaps someone who is more familiar with this kind of world. The audiences range, as you know, from occasional theatregoers to rich patrons. As for Lilias...'

Her finger prodded the fifth handbill, which was quite different in format. Whereas the others had been enhanced with colour, this was in plain black and white.

Lilias Cadwalader, a normal-seeming woman in a sleeveless dark dress, sat in a chair. She could have been any age from twenty to fifty. Instead of the intense stare of Vitruvius, Aelfrida, Ludolphus and Bassalissa, her expression was soft, resigned, as if she wept inwardly. On either side of her stood a shadowy figure draped in cloth, their faces lowered. Three vignettes were placed around her. Lilias, in apparent distress, holding a bundle wrapped in white. Lilias, her eyes closed with smoke emitting from her mouth. Lilias gripping the hands of others sitting at a round table, her head thrown back and her eyes wide. She would take on all your grief and doubt. She would find you answers on the other side.

'The Chelsea Medium,' said Mina. 'We'll leave you till last. But we'll get to you.' She stabbed the handbill again with her finger and her voice dropped to a murmur. 'For Andrew's sake I'll get you. If it's the last thing I do. I'll get you.'

Chapter 8
Connie

The newspaper lowered, revealing Albert's alarmed face. 'You're going to do *what?*'

'I'm going to consult a fortune-teller,' I said, as calmly as I could. 'It's for work.'

'For work,' he repeated, looking dazed.

'Yes,' I said, as if it was the most normal thing in the world. 'We're investigating various mediums and mesmerists for tax purposes, and of course we need to see them at work. So that we can ascertain if they're making extra income which they aren't declaring.'

'Connie…' Albert began to run his hands through his hair, but clutched it, looking anguished at me. 'Whatever will people think?'

'That's why I waited until breakfast was cleared to tell you. Anyway, lots of people we know do that sort of thing. Maisie Frobisher recommended her.'

'You don't believe any of that rubbish, do you?' He

looked half-puzzled, half-frightened.

I laughed. 'Of course not. That's why it's important that I go. If these people are bamboozling the public, they ought to be stopped.'

Slowly Albert took his hands out of his hair, and smoothed it back. 'I see that. But…' His brow furrowed again. 'When are you going?'

'Tonight. I've made a private appointment with her for eight o'clock.'

'Please tell me you haven't used your real name.'

'Of course not. I wrote as Miss Fleet, care of the Oxford Street post-office.'

'Good.' He paused, as if he was not sure how to proceed. 'And where is it?'

'Wandsworth. I believe some of it's quite nice. Mr William Thackeray lived there.'

That news didn't impress Albert as much as I hoped it would. He sat silent for a while, running his finger along the grain of the table.

'Connie, I know this is important to you —'

'And you don't want me to go.'

'No, I don't.' His eyes met mine.

'We made an agreement.' I held his gaze. 'That's why I'm telling you this. I promised not to keep secrets, or to go behind your back. I promised to tell everyone I was engaged in voluntary work. And I've kept my part of the bargain.'

'Yes.' He sighed. 'But you also promised to try not to embarrass yourself, or me. I hate the thought of someone we know seeing you, and thinking you're consulting a fortune-teller. You know how these things get around.'

'I do.' Suddenly a thought struck me. 'I think I have the answer.' I reached across the table and took his hand. 'If you're worried about people seeing me, I'll go as someone else.'

***

'Ain't she a picture?' said Selina. 'You can 'ave a butcher's now, if you like.'

'Should I?' I asked Katherine.

Her expression didn't reassure me. 'You certainly look, um, different. I wouldn't have recognised you.'

'I suppose that's what matters.' I opened my eyes, and started at the black-haired, thick-eyebrowed, over-rouged woman in the mirror. 'Oh dear.'

'It'll all come off with a couple of dabs of cold cream,' said Selina.

'A couple of jars, more like,' said Katherine. 'Anyway, we must go or you'll be late.'

'And so will I,' said Selina, getting up and twitching a spangled costume from the rack. 'I've been so busy beautifying you that I haven't even got dressed.' She grinned. 'Let me know how it goes.'

I pulled down my veil as I left the dressing room. The thought of being recognised under the paint and rouge by anyone who knew me was horrifying.

'Would you like one of us to come with you?' Katherine asked, as we approached the carriage — not our carriage, but one hired from a nearby mews.

I desperately wanted to say yes, but I couldn't. If I

was asserting my right to some independence, then clinging to Katherine or Selina was a bad start. 'No, I'll be fine. It doesn't need a group of us, and besides, I have Tredwell.'

'I suppose.' Katherine sounded rather regretful. 'Make sure you tell me all about it tomorrow.'

'Oh, I shall.' I climbed into the carriage. 'I'll probably still have black eyebrows, too.'

'Good luck,' Katherine murmured. She stepped back and waved as the carriage creaked into movement, until I couldn't see her any more.

I spent most of the journey muttering to myself, rehearsing the questions I planned to ask. I tried to change my voice a little, to modify its pitch and cadence. Under the large bonnet I had procured as further disguise the wig itched, and I did not dare to scratch or touch it in case the whole thing came off. I was almost glad when the carriage slowed down. 'We're coming into the road, ma'am,' called Tredwell.

'Can you stop a little way past the house, please?' I asked. Even in a borrowed carriage, with Tredwell heavily muffled in scarf and cap, I didn't want to run the smallest risk of recognition.

I looked out of the window. Before me was a neat, respectable little row of terraced houses. I wasn't sure what I had expected, but it wasn't this. I squared my shoulders, and descended. 'Wait here, please. I don't expect to be longer than half an hour. If I am, come and fetch me. It's number eight.'

'Number eight,' Tredwell repeated. 'Right you are,

ma'am.'

There was nothing else I could request, no more to say. All there was to do now was knock, and wait.

***

The door was opened by a small girl of about seven, who looked up at me in a very self-contained way. 'Are you 'ere for Bassalissa?'

'I am, yes,' I replied.

'Miss Fleet, innit?' She opened the door to admit me, and I stepped into a narrow hallway. 'If you'd like to wait in the parlour, I'll go an' tell her you're here.' She indicated the first door on the right, and ran upstairs.

I felt unaccountably nervous about opening the parlour door, as if I might release a lion. I inched it open, peeped in, and gasped. The room was hung with red drapery, like something from the Arabian Nights. The gaslight was turned low, and supplemented by a battery of flickering candles on the mantelpiece. But my eyes were drawn to the middle of the room, which held two plain wood chairs, a small table, and on it, a crystal ball.

I sat, and waited. I considered leaving. I could get up, walk out, and go home. I could return to the theatre, clean myself up there, and then go home, which would probably be wiser. But some small sense of duty, of not letting Katherine, or indeed myself down, kept me there.

It could only have been a few minutes before the door opened and a slim, veiled woman slipped in, wearing a robe which might have been a dressing-gown. 'Good evenin',' she murmured. 'Miss Fleet, I believe.'

'That's right,' I said.

'And you want to see into the future.'

I nodded.

'Sure?' She put the veil back, and pale green eyes twinkled at me.

'Of course I'm sure,' I said.

'Ah, but you don't know what the future holds…' She put her hands on the crystal ball for a moment, then looked up at me. 'Would you mind putting your veil up, Miss Fleet? I like to know who I'm talking to.' Her voice was brisk, matter-of-fact, not suspicious at all. I raised it carefully, draping it over my bonnet. 'That's better.' She held out a small, freckled hand. 'Now you just 'ave to cross my palm with silver, an' we'll begin.'

'Oh yes, of course,' I said, opening my bag. I put a florin in her hand. 'Will that do?'

'A shilling is what I meant,' she said, smiling, handing it back. I rummaged in my purse and made a mental note to report that to the office. 'And now I'll 'ave a look at yours, if you don't mind.'

'My hand?'

'Yes,' she said, rather impatiently. 'I'll start by reading your palm.'

I peeled off my left glove, and offered my palm for inspection. Bassalissa leaned over, and her coins jangled in a way that set my teeth on edge.

'I see a long lifeline, an' the possibility of health, wealth and happiness, but you've got a chain on your heart. And your hand is a water hand; everything you feel makes you flow first one way, then the other. You ain't settled.'

I swallowed. She had got closer to me than I cared to admit.

'But that ain't all. I ain't shown you your future. Do you still want me to?' Her sharp green eyes sized me up.

I didn't want her to. But I had to, for the sake of the assignment. 'Yes,' I said, and my voice didn't sound like my own.

'Awright. You'll 'ave to cross my palm again. One coin, one hand.'

I fumbled, and pressed another shilling into her hand, almost dropping it.

'Thank you.' She pocketed it. 'Now, I'll be honest with you, because you seem like a nice person, Miss Fleet. Only it ain't *Miss* Fleet, is it?' Her eyes twinkled, and her finger traced the faint impression at the base of my ring finger.

'My husband didn't want me to come,' I whispered.

'No.' She ran her finger along my hand. 'You've taken all your rings off to come and see me, now ain't that strange.' She turned my hand over gently. 'It's a soft hand, too, and well cared for. That old bonnet don't match your lovely cloak, neither.' Her voice dropped to a murmur. 'What are you up to?'

'I'm not — I'm not up to anything,' I stammered.

'Oh yes you are,' she muttered, leaning forward. 'I saw the minute I came through that door that you weren't my usual clientele. I get shop-girls, I get 'ousemaids, I get idle rich women, and they ain't that much different. They all want to know if they'll get a man, or if they'll keep the man they've got. Sometimes men come, but with them it's about money; an investment, or a will. But they've all got a question. So, *Miss Fleet*, wot are you doing here?'

'I told you,' I said. 'I came to learn my future.'

Bassalissa smiled. 'All right. 'Ere it is.' Her grip on my hand tightened a fraction. 'You're a lady, anyone can see that, and you were telling the truth when you said your husband didn't want you to come. But you don't want to learn your future, even if you tell me that till you're blue in the face.' Her eyes met mine, and she grinned. 'Red, more like, and your face don't match your hands at all. An' if that ain't a wig, I'm a Dutchman.'

'It's as real as yours,' I shot back.

She laughed. 'That's as may be,' she said. 'I only do that cos it's what people expect. Now, if you were got up like that because of your husband, you'd never have bothered to take your rings off. You're dressed like that so I won't recognise you if I see you again. I ain't stupid. You're here to learn about me, not you. Gawd knows why.' Her eyes twinkled. 'Unlike you, I ain't got nothin' to hide.' She looked down at my right hand, still gloved. 'Now if you want your money's worth, you'll need to take off that glove.'

'You were right,' I muttered. 'I don't want to learn my future.'

She sat back, arms folded, as I stood up. 'You're younger than you seem, and smarter than you think. You're doing something your husband don't approve of, yet it matters to you enough to paint your face an' take your jewels off. But you're jumpy as a jackrabbit, cos it don't come natural. You're getting into things you maybe ain't ready for, an' I can't tell why. This I can tell you, though; you'd better watch out. Cos from the look on your face, you're playin' a very dangerous game, and it might not be a game at all.'

'I must go,' I muttered. I ran to the door, and fled.

CHAPTER 9
Katherine

It was Sunday afternoon. James was seeing if he could pull my hairpins out faster than I could replace them. He said it took his mind off other things he could be doing in the ten minutes we were allowed alone in Father's study in view of our engaged status. I was just about winning.

'It will be strange to live in a proper house again,' he said. 'I wish you could come and live in rooms with me. Just the two of us.'

I wasn't quite sure how I felt. In the same way that James couldn't imagine having people round him every meal-time and evening, I couldn't imagine life without them. A year ago, I'd have said 'When Father comes home, I'll move away.' But I had come to accept that he wasn't coming back. Eventually he would be declared dead. I presumed that Margaret and I would inherit, and our lives could go whichever way we wanted them to.

But for now, Margaret and the house were my responsibility. I sighed.

'I'm sorry,' he said. 'I'm being unfair.'

'We could always put the wedding off till after Margaret goes to Somerville in the autumn,' I suggested, making my face very solemn.

He took five hairpins out in one go and my hair fell down over one ear.

'Ow! Stop it! We'll stick to April.' I sat on his lap and kissed him.

'There were seven of us originally,' he said, out of nowhere.

'Seven who?'

'Seven children. Evangeline and I were the youngest. Only one of the others lived beyond eight years old: Reuben. He was the one before Evangeline. He died when I was three. Poor Mother.'

I thought of Connie's sister Jemima. Even if she survived, there was no guarantee the baby would, no matter how coddled they both were.

'My mother lost at least one baby too,' I said.

'Are you worried?'

I shrugged. The answer was 'yes', and the answer was also 'I'm not sure I want a baby at all'. I wasn't sure how to put it in words or ask how he felt. Babies were an inevitability. Unless they weren't.

'Mmm,' James hugged me tight and kissed my cheek. 'Maybe we won't have to worry for a while. Anyway, that wasn't what I wanted to talk about. Not now.'

'My goodness, you're blushing,' I said. 'I didn't know you knew how.'

'Shh. I wanted to tell you something else. About Evangeline.'

'Oh.' I had waited for two weeks. It had cost every ounce of patience I had not to dig, but I knew he had to pick his own moment to explain.

'She had convulsions when she was a baby, but that is common enough, apparently. They stopped. Then when I was very small, I asked Mother why Evangeline kept falling asleep with her eyes open. I thought she was visiting angels. I still don't know if she was daydreaming, or whether the doctors are right about the epilepsy.'

'Oh. I see.'

'When she was nineteen, Evangeline fell from her bedroom window. She was so badly concussed they thought she'd die. It was all a bit of a scandal.'

'A scandal? Why?'

'It happened just before a kitchen maid was dismissed by cook. She told everyone Evangeline had jumped. There was talk of a failed love affair, sinful despair . . . you can imagine. There was no real proof, but — you know what people are like.'

'Yes.'

'While Evangeline recovered, the police called to decide whether she should be prosecuted for attempted suicide, and demanded an interview. She was still badly concussed, and while she was being questioned, she had terrible convulsions. Our old fool of a doctor suggested a lunatic asylum, but my parents refused. She hasn't had a single fit since, that I know of. But everyone is still afraid. There's never been any mention of anyone else in the family suffering from fits, but it's what Geraldine feared was hereditary. I thought I ought to make it clear that it's a possibility. Not that I believe it myself.'

I kissed the top of his head.

'That must have been so hard to tell me,' I said. 'But nothing makes any difference. I'm not letting you go now. I loved you from the first time I kissed you.'

'You hussy.'

I giggled. He kissed my neck, then sighed. 'It's a shame but Father and Mother won't let Evangeline come to the wedding. I've tried, but they won't change their minds. Now let's change the subject.'

He pulled me closer and I ran my finger round his mouth. 'Can you grow a moustache by Thursday?' I asked.

'I can try. It won't be up to its previous luxuriance. Are you missing it?'

'Now you sound like Connie.' I snuggled closer. 'Speaking of whom, Albert will be here to talk about Margaret's university expenses any minute — he said his father wants to get it all straight in advance. I wasn't clear if he was bringing Connie.'

'I have a feeling they're walking on eggshells with each other at the moment,' said James. 'Any idea what's wrong?'

'Not exactly. Perhaps you can talk to Albert when they arrive.'

'It would be easier to grow a moustache by tea-time.'

I shook my head. 'Men are hopeless.'

'Why Thursday?' James asked.

'I have a private viewing with The Great Ludolphus.'

'If you're desperate for conjuring tricks, I could do some for you. When we saw him on stage last night he was very impressive, but I bet face to face he's no better than me.'

'It's not conjuring I'm interested in, it's alchemy.'

'I'd better come in case he decides to cut you in half. No-one is getting you into a small enclosed space but me.'

There was a rap on the study door, then it burst open and Albert peered round.

'Shenanigan Inspector!' he said. 'Put that woman down, King. You don't know where she's been.'

***

In the office the following morning, Connie spilt tea as she sipped.

'I'm all fingers and thumbs,' she said. 'I'm useless.'

'No you're not,' said Mina. 'You're still upset by your visit to Bassalissa the other day. You did an excellent job, and gave a clear and concise report.'

'I can't even visit a fake gypsy without getting it wrong.'

'Who says you got it wrong?'

'She knew I wasn't who I said I was. She saw right through me.'

'It's her bread and butter,' argued Mina. 'A woman who wears a disguise professionally will spot an amateur a mile off.'

'What was I supposed to do? Be myself?'

'I don't know,' said Mina. 'I imagine most people go with a false name so you must have bothered her. You may have done better than you fear.'

'Maybe she recognised you from the illustrated papers. I'll have an advantage tonight,' I said. 'I'm quite anonymous. No-one ever puts my photograph in the society columns.'

Connie groaned. 'Oh, and I looked so miserable in that picture they published.'

'We've run out of biscuits,' said Mina. 'I'll go and buy some, let you talk.'

Connie put her head on her desk, and I could hear the tears in her voice. '*A chain round your heart,* that's what Bassalissa said. How did she know?'

I put my arms round her shoulders.

'That's precisely why we're doing this investigation,' I said. 'She's made you miserable on purpose. Think how you presented yourself. If you had been Bassalissa, what would you have seen?'

'In the crystal ball?'

'No, across the table.'

'Oh.' Connie thought. 'She'd have seen a young woman in disguise who's taken off her wedding ring. I should never have removed my gloves. Awkward, clumsy, stupid…'

'You're none of those. Keep thinking; put yourself in her shoes. What did she see?'

She closed her eyes. 'Shy, nervous . . . guilty. Albert

thought everything was simple and straightforward. And a bit silly. I thought so too at first, but then she said I had a chain round my heart.'

'Which means?'

'It means . . . I don't know. I just saw myself being dropped into the sea and dragged down.'

'That's such a cruel thing to say. You'd go back, wouldn't you? You'd go back to find a solution, go back and pay her more money…'

'I…'

'It meant nothing. She was reacting to your guilt and sowed a seed for you to return.'

'I'm worried,' she said, lifting her head and wiping her eyes. 'I'm worried about how Ludolphus will make you feel.'

'The things on my mind are quite different. I'm sure I'll be fine. Have you told Albert what happened?'

'Not exactly.'

'What's wrong with the two of you?'

'I'm a disappointment to him.'

'Oh, Connie. Of course you're not.'

'He leaves me on my own. He won't confide. He looks at dinner as if it's poisoned. Admittedly it is pretty terrible. Cook can't cook.'

'Borrow Ada for an evening. She'll sort out your cook. Or why not meet Albert for lunch somewhere? Somewhere the food's even worse. Sit down. Talk.'

'It's easy for you to say. It's all different once you're married.'

***

It was hard to put the conversation out of my mind. Connie and Albert needed their heads banging together again. Knowing we would never be so foolish, I squeezed James's arm as we walked up a neat suburban path to a small detached villa called 'Auric Lodge'. It stood between 'Rose Villa' and 'Magnolias' and was the home of The Great Ludolphus. A manservant ushered us into a back parlour. I had expected it to be as dark as Connie had described Bassalissa's, with heavy drapes and thick velvet, but the curtains were open to display a twilit garden and the hissing of gas lamps filled the air as soft yellow light illuminated brass ornaments and crystalware.

We sat on the edge of a small sofa and looked at each other. James's false moustache had been glued on with great precision. He wore the good-quality suit of a chief clerk, neither his own wealthy man's clothes nor the rough sort he wore when undercover. I was dressed in a cornflower-blue dress and black jacket, still quite fashionable. I had dressed my hair in a different style and covered it in a brown net to tone down its colour. We looked respectable and comfortable.

Ludolphus entered, still in a mix of eastern and western clothing, but this time without the turban. 'Good evening Miss Caster, Mr Smith,' he said, bowing. 'Ludolphus Roscoe at your service.'

He took a seat opposite us. 'So, how may I help you? I'm assuming you don't want to be cut in half just before you're spliced.' He chuckled. I felt James's leg twitch next to mine.

'Ah, now you're wondering how I knew that. I have to tell you, my dear Miss Caster, that even those of us with the gift use common-sense as a sort of parlour trick. You are clearly not siblings, you're sitting close together and have an intensity of bearing which suggests a longing not yet met . . . and yet anticipated to be met very soon. I apologise if I'm making you blush, Miss Caster. I prefer to explain right at the outset that I am an observant man, so that you know what is real and what is not. Aha, here's Davis.'

The manservant had entered silently. He put a crystal jug of water and some wine glasses on a low table, then withdrew. Ludolphus poured water from the clear jug into the glasses and they brimmed with a rich red fluid. The scent of dark berries filled the air.

'Water into wine,' said Ludolphus. 'I suspect Mr Smith knows how that's done.' He handed us a glass each and raised a toast. 'To alchemy. That's why you're here, isn't it Miss Caster?'

I found my voice. 'I'm just so very interested,' I said. 'I've always been fascinated by the mysterious, but I also have an interest in science. Naturally I haven't had a great deal of opportunity to experiment myself, although Mr Smith does promise he will fit out a little laboratory all of my own when we're married.'

'Does he now?' said Ludolphus, sipping his wine. 'And you'd like to learn ancient secrets to try for yourself.'

'Well, obviously,' I said. 'I don't imagine it's that easy to do, otherwise there would be no mystery. I am just curious.' The wine was going to my head, and I hoped I wasn't slurring.

'But if you could turn cheap metal into gold it would be so helpful, wouldn't it? A wedding is hard to organise, especially on your own.'

'Yes.' My head was spinning now, and images of menus and our little stove whirled through my mind, faster and faster. I tried to make a joke. 'Do you suppose cheese sandwiches would do for a wedding breakfast? I'm not the best cook. Only —' I dropped my voice to a whisper, 'don't tell my fiancé.'

James reached over, took the glass from my hand and put it with his on the tray.

'Let the dog see the rabbit, Roscoe,' he said. 'How do you turn lead into gold?'

'Oh it takes time, Mr Smith. Time and wisdom. I have to channel the force, you see. I have to know how much is needed, and why. I must be sure that the recipient will only use it for good. I am particularly interested in orphans, and the . . . abandoned.' He lifted my glass from the tray, tipped the contents back into the jug, and then poured out again. This time, it was clear water flowing into my glass.

'I believe I can help you, Miss Caster. You must trust in me, and I shall tell you what to do. Then you needn't take money from an inheritance which isn't quite yours ever again.'

My blood ran cold. How on earth did he know?

Chapter 10
Connie

The journey back from my meeting with Bassalissa had been possibly the worst of my life so far. I had instructed Tredwell to return to the music hall by an indirect route, and spent my time in alternately huddling in the corner of the carriage and in leaning out of the window to see if we were being followed. I saw nothing suspicious; but still I shivered. What if — what if, somehow, Bassalissa was following me home, and she managed to get into the house and cause a scene? I couldn't imagine what Albert's reaction might be. I longed to cry out my fears; but the thought of adding a black-smeared face to the mess I already was made me chew my bottom lip and dig my nails into my palms.

At the music hall I ran past Ron without even a greeting, straight to the dressing-room. There were a few cries at my hasty entrance; but luckily Selina was there. 'It's all right girls, it's only Miss Fleet in a getup,' she said, grinning. 'Someone after you?'

'I hope not,' I said, pulling off my bonnet and dropping it on the floor. The black wig I had borrowed went the same way. I looked at myself in the foxed dressing-table mirror; a near-hysterical woman with hair pinned tight to her head and eyebrows that made no sense at all. Only then did I begin to cry.

'Bad performance?' asked Selina, sympathetically.

'In a manner of speaking, yes,' I sniffled.

'Never mind.' She came to sit by me, and took a jar of cream from the table. ''Ere, let me do it. You're shaking so much you'll 'ave your own eye out.' Once she had finished cleaning me up, I made her inspect me for traces of 'Miss Fleet' three times before I redid my hair, resumed the bonnet, and went back outside.

'Home, ma'am?' Tredwell asked, yawning.

'Yes, please,' I said, climbing up.

'Usual route?'

I looked up and down the street. 'I think so.'

'Good. Master'll be worried. Gee-up!' he said to the horses, and we rattled away.

I spent the journey home anticipating an evening of angry questions. The thought was more than I could stand, after the battering I had already received from Bassalissa. The chain she had seen round my heart tightened until I felt as if I would suffocate.

'Pleasant evening, ma'am?' asked Johnson.

'Yes, thank you.' I began to remove my bonnet before reflecting that my hair probably looked nothing like it had earlier. 'Where is Mr Lamont?' I asked.

'He's in the study, ma'am. I'm about to bring supper, if you'd like some.'

'Perhaps a little something,' I said, though I felt too sick to eat. I walked down the passage like a condemned criminal, and tapped at the door.

I had expected to find Albert at the desk, bent over papers; but he was lounging in the armchair reading a novel. 'Connie!' He put the book aside, got up, and kissed me. 'You're back, and . . . you smell a bit peculiar,' he said, drawing away a little.

'It's only cold cream,' I said. 'If you recall, I did say I'd attend the session as someone else.'

'So you did. That explains this monstrosity,' he said, removing my bonnet. 'Good heavens, what's happened here?' he said, laughing and running his hand over my hair.

'I had to pin it down for a wig,' I said, shortly. 'You try doing your own hair when it's past your waist.'

'I suppose.' He glanced at me, and his smile transformed into a look of concern. 'Are you all right? Nothing — happened, did it?'

'No, no,' I assured him, trying to smile so that his would return. 'She — said a few things, but it doesn't matter. She'll never see me again.'

'What sort of things?' Trust Albert to pin down the very thing I'd hoped he wouldn't.

'She knew I was married, because she felt the indentation where my ring would be. And she knew I wasn't what I pretended to be. She was very observant. I don't think it was any more than that,' I said firmly.

'And I don't think she's a fraudster. Her rates are far too reasonable.'

'Good. I do worry, you know —'

A knock at the door. 'Supper's here, sir,' called Johnson. 'Shall I come in?'

'Not quite yet,' I called back, snatching my bonnet and jamming it on my head. 'Now you can.'

Johnson opened the door to find me glaring at Albert, who was convulsed with laughter. 'Supper, sir, and two plates,' he said, setting the tray on the desk and vanishing.

'I am not eating supper with you wearing that thing.' Albert twitched it off and held it out of reach. I thought about jumping for it, but decided that the noise might summon Johnson.

'All right,' I said, sitting in the armchair. 'You can admire my untidy hair instead.'

'I'd rather not,' Albert said, dropping the bonnet and crossing the room to kneel at my feet. 'I'd rather do this.' He kissed me, and, running his fingers through my hair, started to remove the pins.

'Ooh,' I gasped between kisses. 'Not fair!' And then I stopped caring.

***

'Telegram for — you, ma'am,' said Johnson, double-checking the envelope before he handed it over.

Albert raised his eyebrows as I used my butter-knife to open the flap, then raced through the contents. 'Well?'

'It's from Katherine,' I said, smiling at his eager face.

'Her visit to our next, um, person of interest has gone well.'

Katherine had written: *Fun night out with J and charlatan coming at 9 to give you gist K.*

'She does sound excited,' Albert commented, passing the telegram back to me. 'Johnson, you can stand down for a bit. We'll ring if we need you.'

Johnson goggled. 'Very good, sir,' he said, exiting the room backwards.

I tried to look nonchalant, but curiosity got the better of me. 'Why did you dismiss Johnson?' I half-mouthed.

Albert looked bashful. 'Well, it's almost nine o'clock now, and . . . I wanted to ask you if I could sit in on your meeting.' He put a forkful of greyish scrambled egg into his mouth, grimaced and swallowed. 'I'd invite K to breakfast, but she wouldn't thank us.'

I regarded him over the rim of my teacup. 'Are you sure you want to know what we're up to?'

Albert set his knife and fork neatly in the middle of his half-finished breakfast, and pushed the plate away. 'I feel I should.'

***

We were still in the morning room when Katherine arrived. Johnson hovered in the doorway, anxious-faced. 'Miss Demeray is here. Shall I put her in the drawing room?'

'We can see her in here,' I said, and I felt rather than saw Albert's look. 'Would you mind clearing, Johnson? And could you ask Mrs Jones for a fresh pot of tea and an extra cup, please.'

'Does that mean I can stay?' Albert asked, leaning across the table and taking my hand.

I nodded, though I was not at all sure I wanted him to. I just hoped Katherine would be circumspect. This last week, Albert had seemed calmer, happier, less quick to anger; but I did not want to tempt fate.

She came in all smiles. 'Are you ready for a tale of fakery the like of which you have never heard before?' she said, spreading her hands. I shot her a warning look, but I might as well not have bothered.

'Do stop it, K,' said Albert. 'You're not on stage.'

Katherine sat down at the table. 'He was just a conjuror,' she said. 'James and I went round, and he had a sort of magic jug which poured wine if you tipped it one way and water if you tipped it the other, but in the end all he could come up with was a lot of mumbo-jumbo.' She snorted. 'Buy this magic crystal,' she intoned, waggling her fingers in the air. 'Purchase this elixir to realise riches beyond your wildest dreeeeams…'

'You didn't, did you?' Albert asked, frowning.

'Don't be ridiculous. I'd have considered it so that we could get them analysed, but not at those prices.' She paused as Johnson came in with a tray, and I saw her impatience in her twitching fingers.

'So nothing — odd happened?' I asked, once he had gone.

Katherine laughed. 'Nooo. It was nothing like your experience, Connie. I didn't even need James, really —'

'Wait, what?' Albert swung round to look at me.

'But you said —'

'It was fine,' I said, resisting the urge to glare at Katherine. 'I told you. Bassalissa made a few lucky hits, and that unsettled me at the time, but when I came home, and you were there, I felt quite all right.' That was true but in a limited sense, since Bassalissa's words haunted me at least once a day.

'Mm.' Albert didn't look convinced. 'If I'd known that James was going to accompany K, I wouldn't have let you go alone. I think you should at least go in pairs from now on.'

'Perhaps you're right,' I said.

'It depends on the fraudster, Albert,' Katherine said, leaning to put her elbows on the table. 'Sometimes a couple is more convincing, or a woman on her own. They won't try to take advantage of us if they think there's a witness. That's the whole point.'

I had learnt some choice language backstage at the music hall, but I had never wanted to use it as much as I did in that moment.

'You want them to take advantage of you,' Albert sounded dazed.

'No! Not like that!' I cried. 'We're investigating them to see if they're exploiting people! You know, making them think they can speak to their dead husband, that sort of thing, to get money out of them. Not the other thing, not at all!'

'Much as it pains me to do as I'm told,' said Katherine, 'maybe two of us will manage the next visit. Tea, anyone?' We both stared as she poured a stream of very pale liquid into her cup. 'Or...'

'That is IT!' I shouted. I pulled the pot towards me and removed the lid. Inside, a bare sprinkling of tea-leaves was visible. I leapt up and rang the bell. 'Take that away,' I growled when Johnson appeared. 'I asked for tea, not hot water.'

'Have I come at a bad time?' asked Katherine, when the footman had scurried off, bearing the pot in front of him as if it might explode.

'Just everyday life at the Lamont household,' Albert replied. 'Conspiracy, magic tricks, secret agents, and abominable food.' His shoulders began to shake, and I realised he was laughing. 'But at least it's fun.'

***

'I'm a bit worried about Katherine,' I confided, once she had gone.

'I'm always worried about Katherine,' Albert reached across the sofa and took my hand. 'Why now, particularly?'

I sighed. 'She seemed so insistent that everything was fine last night.'

Albert shrugged. 'Maybe her one wasn't as scary as yours.'

'Maybe. I think she was trying to convince herself, not me.'

Albert traced the lines on my palm with his forefinger. 'Don't,' I said, pulling it away.

'She really disturbed you, didn't she?' His voice was soft.

'I'll get over it,' I said, as bravely as I could. And

provided Albert wasn't angry or cold, I thought I would.

'I hope so. May I?' I nodded, and he drew me to him. 'I need to say something. No, not in that way,' he said, as he felt me stiffen. 'I've been — moody lately, I know I have. Father's been difficult.'

'I know.'

'I told you about the money thing, but there's been more. Lectures on how I have to be responsible now I'm married. Keep a good house, entertain, be seen with the right people in the right places.' His voice was edged with bitterness. 'All this while he's investing in hare-brained schemes, of course.'

'Oh Albert, you should have told me.'

'I should. But you were moping, and the food —'

'Oh, the food…' I looked up at him. 'If it doesn't improve very soon, I'll give her notice. That tea was the last straw.'

'It was, rather. And watching you being miserable, and not knowing what to do —'

'I'll try to be better.'

'No! *They* must be better. Anyway.' He stroked my hair. 'Father seems better. You seem better. When you came back from your — outing — you were so glad to see me. I don't ever want you to be sorry to see me. That's what it's felt like lately, and it's been my fault.'

The stroking continued, as if Albert was working himself up to the next bit. 'And?' I prompted.

He sighed. 'I thought there might be a little more behind your job than tax evasion. I want you to be honest with me, Connie. And I don't want you to put yourself in danger; these magicians and crystal-gazers don't sound like particularly nice people. So please promise me that you'll be careful. If that means taking me with you, that's what we'll do.'

I snuggled closer. 'Are you sure this isn't just because you don't want to miss the excitement?' I whispered.

Albert held up a hand and waggled his fingers, much as Katherine had done. 'You see right through me, young lady,' he declaimed, and tickled me till I begged for mercy.

CHAPTER 11
Katherine

'I wouldn't wear that,' said Mina, adjusting her hat and pinning an amethyst brooch to her brown herringbone jacket. As usual, she was neat, efficient and smart, but I was surprised she had picked her dullest clothes.

'What's wrong with it?' I looked down at myself. I had dressed in my favourite suit of soft green with its intricate black trim and tiny jet buttons. Everyone said how well the colour suited me . . . except James, who complained that the buttons stabbed him when he hugged me.

'Cats,' said Mina. 'She's bound to have cats. You'll get covered in fur and it'll take a month of Sundays to brush off. Put on your tweed. The fur won't show up on that.'

'Oh, but I look so drab in the tweed... James might come round later.'

'I'm sure James won't like you fluffy. Trust me.

There will be cats.'

Half an hour later we met Selina at Earl's Court. The underground was stuffy, and the fact that it was drizzling outside and everyone's damp clothes steamed in the carriage didn't help.

'Where to, Miss C?' said Selina. I had almost walked past her at Earl's Court. Instead of being peacock-bright and painted, she wore grey and was pale-faced. I hadn't known until now that she had freckles.

'Acton,' said Mina. 'There's still rather a way to go. Thank you for coming with us.'

Selina grinned. 'Thanks for asking me. Quite an adventure, this. Acton sounds sorta dramatic. Right place for a performer, eh? What's Acton like, Miss C?'

'I've no idea,' I said.

'I'd have liked to wear something fancy for coming out west, but you know,' Selina said as we boarded the next train, 'she's bound to 'ave cats.'

They were right. Aelfrida did have cats.

The first was a young, lithe ginger tom glaring from beneath a shrub as we approached the front door, as if the rain was all our fault.

We were admitted into the narrow hallway by a plump maid wearing a sort of Grecian robe and goose-pimples, and found ourselves under observation by two matronly tortoiseshells. They watched us from the staircase with unblinking eyes and their tails flicked as we were ushered into the parlour, which was full of oak furniture and pot-plants. A ball of kittens on the rug stopped fighting and shot under various pieces of furniture, including the sofa we sat on. Amongst the trailing ferns on the piano, an elderly white Persian sat up straight and turned opaque eyes on us.

We waited. There was a jangle of bells, and somewhere a music box began to tinkle out a tune.

Aelfrida wafted in wearing diaphanous blue, silk flowers adorning her mass of titian curls. In her arms was a small grey tabby. The room was a little dim, with its thick lace curtains and forest-green walls, but I swear the cat smirked. She gave out a tiny mew, and what felt like a million needles pierced my calf.

I let out a scream. Every kitten rushed from its hiding place and ricocheted around the walls and furniture like bullets.

'Welcome,' said Aelfrida in solemn tones. 'The magic is upon us.'

She drifted across the room as if on wheels, and sat on what I had thought was an oversized floral display but turned out to be a frond-draped chaise longue. She reclined, tucking herself among the foliage. The cat strolled with dainty paws along the green velvet, batted a dangling bloom unknown to botany, then curled up on Aelfrida's shins, pulling her skirt awry to reveal lumpy veined feet encased in silver slippers.

'Welcome,' she repeated, wincing a little as the music juddered to a halt and was replaced by the sound of someone, presumably the maid, muttering as she wound the box up again.

There was silence for a moment before the music recommenced. It was unnerving, and I opened my mouth without any idea what I was going to say. Mina trod on my foot and I closed my mouth again. Selina had settled on the sofa and was peering round the room. I followed suit. It was predominantly green, with leafy plants and silk flowers everywhere. The furniture was mismatched, dark and covered in stylised ivy, but now that my eyes had adjusted to the lack of light I could see that the carving was poor, as if someone had taken a blunt chisel to items bought from house sales.

When Aelfrida spoke it made me jump. 'I,' she said, 'am Eternal.'

'Comes to us all in the end,' said Selina. 'My mate Betty's fifty if she's a day but you'd never know it. She rubs in a pound of cold cream every night and she can pass for thirty-five in a low light. You should try it. You wouldn't look a day over forty in no time.'

Aelfrida took a deep breath and tossed her curls, which slipped just a little.

'I am of the greenwood; the holly and ivy, the oak and birch. I have forsworn the joys of Fairyland to help those who need to find peace.' She stretched the last word into a soft hiss. 'Peeeeassss.'

'That's kind of you,' said Selina. 'What did you do with your wings?'

'Wings? I . . . they are too delicate to bring into the mortal realm.'

'I'll bet wings're a swine to wash in the bath,' said Selina. 'It's hard enough to do your back. Or do they unclip and —'

I nudged her, less to make her stop than to stop

myself from laughing.

'Thank you for agreeing to meet us, Aelfrida,' said Mina. 'My young friends and I are curious as to what you have to offer us.'

Aelfrida glanced towards Selina and gave a small smile. 'Your maid seems less curious.'

'She could sit with your maid in the kitchen,' I suggested, and Selina gave me a filthy look.

The grey tabby opened one eye and flicked the tip of her tail.

'Oh no,' said Aelfrida, 'that won't be necessary. The gift of hearing the Fair Folk is often not given to those of the lower classes.'

Selina snorted. I was aware of something pulling at my skirt and looked down to see a furry wide-eyed face as one of the kittens pulled itself onto my knee. It paused as we stared at each other, gave a silent mew and finished clambering into my lap where it purred and kneaded my thighs. I felt like a pin cushion.

'Yet even for those of genteel blood, ancient coin must be paid.'

'What's an ancient coin then?' asked Selina, before Mina or I could stop her. 'A groat?'

Aelfrida's jaw clenched slightly. 'No dear, a silver sixpence. Each.'

Mina placed a florin in the bowl indicated. 'I'm sorry, this will have to do. Please keep the extra sixpence for…' she glanced sideways at Selina, 'interruptions to the cosmic flow.'

Aelfrida lay back under the fronds with her eyes

partially closed. The dislodged cat reorganised herself, pulling up more of Aelfrida's skirt to reveal a rather blue ankle. I wondered if Selina was going to suggest that even fairies should wear stockings, but she had sat up straight and put on a demure expression. A low scratchy whispering echoed round the room.

There was a slight movement to my left, but when I turned there was nothing to be seen but an alcove with a bunch of pansies in it. A bell rang above our heads and Aelfrida sat up, cradling the cat against her bosom. Another kitten had clambered onto my lap and begun to climb up my jacket.

'The Fair Folk have spoken from glade and stream,' said Aelfrida. 'Beyond the cataracts where mortals may not go, particularly those with souls of lead and iron.' Her glance flickered towards Selina. 'Where yet my erstwhile companions flutter in rainbow sparkling glades, uncluttered with dwellings and cares —'

'Not Acton, then,' said Selina.

Aelfrida lost her thread but maintained her composure. 'You, my dear madam —' She fixed her gaze on Mina. 'You need not fear that you must sully your hands with toil, provided you are wise in whom you employ.' She looked at Selina again. 'Your riches are secure, and the Fair Folk can direct you as to their investment, and guide you to find a husband. Now, this young lady is another matter.' She turned to me. 'The Fair Folk reveal that you have great sympathy with the fairy kind, for you are descended from elves. Many are the nights you weep into your pillow over the many men who court you. Cast off your natural timidity, your shyness —'

'Your corsets,' whispered Selina.

'Your eyes glisten with maidenly tears,' Aelfrida continued.

It was true. The kitten on my lap was still kneading and the uppermost kitten had made its way to my shoulder, where it was pulling out a hairpin and getting tangled in my curls. I was in agony.

'The suitor you must choose,' said Aelfrida, in low confidential tones, 'is the one who like you is descended from elves: romantic and taciturn, weeping in his manly heart as he yearns to give you roses.' The thought of this as a description of James momentarily distracted me from the kittens. 'Let the Fair Folk bring you together.'

'And as for you,' she said to Selina, 'it seems you may have pixie blood. When you tire of playing the fool and capering on the very edges of decency, they will be ready to guide you, but until then —'

'Ackchally, *playing the fool and capering* pays quite well, and it beats laundry any day, doncher think?' said Selina, rising. 'Any time the Fair Folk decide to improve the staging, let me know. They could do with a few more tunes on their music box, for starters. I'll let myself out, there's some pixies waiting for me south of the river.'

Mina and I followed with as much dignity as we could muster, making apologetic faces at Aelfrida.

'Really, Selina,' said Mina as we settled in the underground train at Mill Hill Park station. 'You're very naughty. My face is hurting from trying to keep straight.'

'She coulda offered us a cuppa, at least,' said Selina. 'All that way and nothing to drink. It pays to know your audience. Still…' she mused, 'with a bit of work, that act'd do well on stage. I'm gonna mention it to Mr T. It'd need someone with a sense of 'umour though. Not sure old Aelf 'as got one. What about you, Miss C? Fancy comin' back?'

I was still laughing. Other passengers were looking sideways at me. I must have looked a sight, tears streaming down my face and hair draggling on one side.

'I'll leave the theatre to the experts,' I giggled. 'I can't wait to tell Connie.'

'Mmm,' said Mina, reaching to pin up my stray curls. 'Well, one thing is for certain. Aelfrida may be a fraud, but I don't think she has the brains to be involved in anything more sinister than getting sixpences from romantics who want to hear nonsense.'

'Nothing wrong with that,' said Selina. 'But the show's got to be worth it. And 'ave less cats. Talking of which, Miss Caster, did you know there's a kitten sleeping on your hat?'

'Is there?' I reached up, dislodging Mina's arm so that more of my hair came down.

Selina screeched with laughter, to the disapproval of the other passengers. 'You oughtn't to be let out, Miss C. But next time you want to do this sorta thing, let me know. It's been the best afternoon I've 'ad for years.'

***

'Oh, to have been a fly on the wall,' said Connie the next day, wiping her eyes.

'Butterfly, I think you mean,' said Mina, smiling.

Connie sobered. 'I wish my experience with Bassalissa had been as much fun.'

'And mine with Ludolphus,' I said, before I could stop myself.

The others stared. I had told them the whole thing, except for the part about the inheritance.

'Do you know what I think is wrong with you two?' said Mina. 'You are both brave but vulnerable. I expected Aelfrida to see in me a woman in her forties, on the shelf, a little impecunious with no prospect of marriage, but she is an amateur. The fact that she read both of us so very wrong means she has nothing to hide.'

'Selina distracted her,' I argued.

'A good medium would have tried to manipulate Selina too. Aelfrida is just a bad actress. But the others are different. They saw the truth and had the chance to use it for good or evil.'

Connie fidgeted, then poked at the typewriter keys.

'Connie, stop worrying,' said Mina. 'Bassalissa saw an anxious woman in disguise who was very unhappy. Now you are content.'

Connie sighed. Mina reached over and gave her hand a squeeze. 'She told you nothing more than the truth. You did have a chain round your heart, but have since found the key. Bassalissa did nothing more than warn you not to waste any more money. Now, Katherine…'

I could still taste the spiced wine.

'He guessed everything about me,' I said.

'He didn't guess anything. You told him. He suggested the "splicing", and if you'd said "oh no, we're half siblings" or something, he'd have said "yet so close" and gone down a different route. But you didn't. Then he suggested you were organising the wedding alone and you confirmed it. Your answers confirmed suggestions.'

'But at the end…'

'Yes. At the end?'

I was supposed to be in charge of this team and here they were harrying me.

'Katherine. You must tell the truth. I know it's a difficult subject, but Connie has been open about her feelings.'

'He knew about the inheritance.'

'What inheritance?' said Connie.

'Mine. Father left a will. It can't come into effect until seven years after his death, but under extreme circumstances I can ask his lawyer for advances against it. I thought about the wedding expenses. It's the bride's family who pay, remember. And I felt . . . I felt dirty and desperate. It's like wishing Father dead, when I never imagined a wedding where he wouldn't walk me down the aisle.' I burst into tears. 'And that man knew. He *knew*.'

'He didn't know,' said Mina. Her arms held me even though I was rigid inside. 'He guessed. It's what he does. Your feelings will have appeared in your face for just long enough. Another woman would buy amulets and crystals and potions to make her pure of heart, so that the alchemy would work. When it didn't, he'd say "one more potion, a different amulet, try this crystal". That's why this sort of person is so evil.'

I swallowed.

'What I think we all need is fresh air.' Mina gathered our hats and gloves. 'We shall take a turn in the park, and I shall tell you about Andrew.'

***

We found a bench in the sun. It was not yet noon and the working crowd were still toiling over counters and desks as we should have been; maidservants were doubtless scrubbing away, while gentlemen were making transactions or waiting for lunch at their clubs. It was very peaceful.

'I want to tell you a story,' said Mina.

I had stopped crying and was fairly sure my eyes were no longer red. I now felt rather foolish, and therefore cross. Connie's earlier contentment had returned. Mina, however, was sober and distant.

'It is short and it is sad, and hitherto, it has been secret. It concerns a man called Andrew Fowler who worked for the Department some years ago.'

'I… Actually I am sure I recall typing his name.'

Mina perused me. 'How curious. In what context?'

'I can't remember,' I said, truthfully.

'Mmm. I met Andrew through a mutual friend, and we struck up a friendship.'

She sighed. A youngish man in office clothes strolled near, pausing to light a pipe. Mina said nothing, but a slight nudge stopped me from asking her to continue.

'Shall we resume our walk, ladies?' She rose and stepped briskly forward, while Connie and I followed in her wake like ducklings.

'Where are we going?' whispered Connie.

'I fancy a visit to the cake shop,' said Mina loudly. 'Oh, did we leave anything behind?' She stopped to check in her bag, then turned.

The man, who had been ambling in our direction, slowed and peered into his pipe.

'Silly me!' said Mina. 'We're heading the wrong way. Perhaps it's my head I left on the bench.'

We retraced our steps. The youngish man was still watching us. I gave him what I hoped was a coquettish smile and dipped my head.

'Well done,' hissed Mina. 'I saw him last night near Aelfrida's. He's up to something.'

We walked through the park gates towards the river. Near the embankment, Mina looked into the river. I shivered, remembering a wet night in November not so long ago. Connie stood with her back to the stonework.

'And then,' said Mina, 'we became lovers.'

She might as well have said they had gone for afternoon tea. It was that matter of fact.

'Did . . . who did . . . how?'

'No one knew. We were very discreet. It wouldn't have happened but for the fact we were very much in love and planned to marry. Andrew had a good job with the Department. He was a widower and had adult stepchildren who worried him. They should have been independent, but were not. A boy who was in debt, a girl who had made a bad marriage. Andrew wanted to provide me with a good home. He settled money to separate himself from the children who had never been in any sense his, but he still felt responsible. He wanted to make peace with his dead wife's spirit, and went to consult Lilias. He asked me to accompany him; I refused. He went again and again, and in the end, I told him to choose a future with me or a past with his dead wife.'

Mina seemed to gather herself for the next words. 'I never saw him again. Two days after our argument, he was run over by an underground train. The coroner ruled it an accident, pure and simple. Bystanders said he seemed feverish and on the point of fainting, and then he fell onto the rail. There was nothing anyone could do. It was not an accident — but I was too lost in grief to think straight.'

'You believe he killed himself?'

'No. I believe he was murdered. And I want to know why he had to die.'

Chapter 12
Connie

'Let's go back to the office.' I put a hand on Mina's arm, but she stood still and rigid as a statue, her eyes fixed on the lapping river as if she expected to see Andrew Fowler in its depths.

'I didn't think it would hurt so much, still,' she whispered, and a tear ran down her cheek. 'I'm sorry.'

'Don't be sorry.' Katherine took her other arm and turned her gently from the river. '*They* should be sorry.'

Mina wiped the tear away, and her face hardened again. 'A walk will do me good.' And she set off at such a pace that we almost had to run to keep up with her.

At the office, we made a pot of tea and then looked at the desks, the piles of paper, the redundant typewriters, and each other. There were so many questions I wanted to ask Mina — so many things that I thought would help us to understand what we were dealing with — but now was not the time.

'I feel helpless,' Katherine said. Her voice was unexpectedly loud in the quiet space.

I looked across at her. She was leaning against her desk, and while she was perfectly neat and tidy — her suit smart, her hair pinned up just as always — there was an air of distraction and disorder about her. 'I know what you mean,' I replied.

'I feel it too,' said Mina. 'And I hate it.'

'It feels as if we're getting nowhere with this. All we're doing so far is making ourselves miserable.' Katherine laughed, but there was no mirth in it. 'By the time we're finished, we'll be nervous wrecks scared of our own shadows.'

'That's how they work,' said Mina, putting an arm round Katherine's shoulders. 'They draw you in, they make you feel that they're the only one who can help, and they isolate you from everyone else, until you're addicted. Until you'd do anything for another message, or manifestation, or whatever fakery they're peddling. Believe me, I know.'

'Then we must stop arranging private meetings with these people,' Katherine said, smacking the desk with the flat of her hand. 'Yes, we're learning how they operate, but we're also exposing ourselves. It's too dangerous. Even James —' Her voice faltered a little, and she looked down for a moment. 'Even James was rattled after our visit to Ludolphus. The wine had gone to my head a little so I can't remember everything Ludolphus said, but yesterday James mentioned that one of Ludolphus's comments might have been about his sister. When I asked what it was, he wouldn't tell me.' Her eyes were wide, and troubled. 'And James is the most sceptical, matter-of-fact person I know.'

'No-one is safe,' said Mina, quietly.

'What are we going to do?' I heard the frustration in my own voice. 'You're right, Katherine; we can't go on like this, but how *can* we go on? How can we put a stop to it all?'

'We know what they're doing, but we need proof of what they've done, and some of the terrible things that have happened as a result.' Katherine said, slowly. 'We need insider information, and we probably won't get it from the victims.'

'We need someone who, with the right incentive, will tell us what they know.' I looked up, and the unoccupied desk, covered with papers, caught my eye. 'Someone who is in the business, but will be honest with us —'

'And where shall we find someone like that?' Katherine asked. 'Selina?'

I closed my eyes, and squeezed them tighter as the horrible feeling I had experienced a few short days ago came back to me. The feeling of being trapped, impaled like a butterfly on a pin, while someone read my innermost thoughts and fears as if I were made of glass. The feeling that layer upon layer of disguise, and pretence, and convention was being stripped away, until there was nothing left at all. 'No. Not Selina. I know exactly where to look.'

***

'Are you sure this is a good idea?' Katherine asked, as the carriage rattled along.

'Honestly?' I looked at her apprehensive face. 'I don't know. But it might work.'

'Maybe I should have got James to come,' she muttered. 'Do you think it's wise to go as ourselves?'

'We can give false names, if you like,' I said. 'But she'd see through any other pretence. Especially in daylight.' I smiled my bravest smile, while my stomach churned.

'Do you want me to go past the house again?' called Tredwell.

'No, you can pull up outside this time.'

It was nine o'clock in the morning, and the fresh, crisp March air fought with my queasiness as I got down from the carriage. Was it my imagination, or did the house look smaller than I remembered? 'Come on,' I said to Katherine, who was hanging back. 'Let's get this over with.' I climbed the steps to number eight, and lifted the brass knocker.

A small, slim woman with bright-red hair peered round the door at me. 'Morning,' she said, frowning. 'Bit early for a social call, ain't it?'

'I thought it would be a good time,' I said. 'As your daughter will be at school.'

'Waved her off half-hour since,' she said, her eyes looking past me before fixing themselves on my face again. 'Anyway. What d'yer want? I don't believe we've met.' The green eyes narrowed. 'Or 'ave we?'

I wanted to pull my jacket tight around myself, but

resisted. 'We have met,' I said. 'But you looked, um, different.'

'So you've met me as Bassalissa,' she said, grinning.

'Yes,' I said. 'That's what we've come about.'

Her eyes flicked to Katherine. 'Have you, indeed. Well, Bassalissa ain't here right now.' She made to shut the door, but I got my foot in the way just in time.

'No, you don't understand! We've come to make you an offer!'

The pressure on my foot eased a little. 'An offer?'

'Yes, an offer.' I leaned in and lowered my voice. 'Of money, for information.'

'I see.' The green eyes took me in, valuing my clothes, pricing me up, until I wanted to squirm. 'You'd better come in.'

***

'Miss Fleet,' Bassalissa repeated, frowning as she scrutinised me. 'I wouldn't have known you. Either you're a better actress than you look, or you've cheered up a lot since our last meeting.'

'You helped,' I said quietly. 'I hated it, but — you were worth the money, ten times over.'

'Good,' she said briskly. 'An' your silent colleague here?'

'Miss Caster,' said Katherine, rather tersely. 'And you are?'

Bassalissa's mischievous grin made her look like a naughty child. 'In the daytime I go by Mrs Bugg. An' yes, that is my real name. If I was gonna make one up, I'd invent a better one.' She opened the parlour door.

The red hangings had disappeared, apart from the window-curtains, and the wooden chairs were supplemented with a couple of small, straight-backed armchairs which reminded me a little of Bassalissa herself. 'Take a seat,' she said. 'D'you want tea first, or are you gonna jump straight in?'

I looked at Katherine, who swallowed, then nodded. 'We'll jump straight in.'

***

'It's a good offer,' Bassalissa said, meditatively. 'And I can still do Bassalissa on the side?'

'Oh yes,' I assured her. 'In fact, I want you to. You're the only honest one we've met, so far. If people are coming to you, hopefully they won't get drawn in by the others.'

'No.' She seemed to be looking at something far, far away. Beyond the room, beyond the house, beyond the street. 'I never used to do this, you know. It's only been since Mr Bugg passed on. I mean to say, I've always been what you call a sharp woman. Like my mother before me.' Her soft expression transmuted to a grin. 'We'd probably've been burned as witches in earlier times.'

'Oh, I'm sure you wouldn't,' I said, hastily, then blushed as her green eyes crinkled up at me.

'I learnt most of what I know through watching Ma. She had a reputation as a wise woman in the village where we lived. People would come to her for advice, an' cures, an' all sorts of things. The doctor hated it, but Ma was a lot cheaper than him.' She snorted. 'And better value, if you ask me. I never thought I'd have to do it myself, you see. I wanted to see the big city, so I went for a scullery maid. I worked up to housemaid, and met Mr Bugg on one of my afternoons off. We was married for five years, an' Tilly was just two when he got taken sudden.' She looked at me, her hands clasped tight in her lap.

'I'm so sorry.' The words dropped like dead leaves.

'I 'ad to do something. Mr Bugg left a bit of savings, but there weren't much more. An' with Tilly so small, I couldn't get a job, not unless I left her with someone all day, an' I couldn't bear that.' She rubbed the corner of her eye, blinked, and continued.

'I was wandering round town one day carrying Tilly, at my wits' end, when I saw a poster for one o' them mind readers. That's how it begun. An' it's done me well. We ain't rich, not by a long chalk, but we're comfortable. The thing is…' She looked up, and her jaw was as set as it had been when she tried to shut the door on me. 'It ain't gonna last for ever. Tilly's seven now, and soon she'll cotton on to what her Ma's doing.' She laughed, but it rang hollow. 'She thinks I'm playing pretend games at the moment, like she plays kings and queens or lords an' ladies with her friends. I want her to grow up respectable. An' this is a start.'

'So . . . you're in?' Katherine asked.

Green eyes met green eyes.

'Let me go over it again,' said Bassalissa. 'Three days a week, in school hours, paid regular.'

I nodded.

'You'll keep me out of it, if it goes to trial.'

'Yes,' said Katherine, leaning forward.

'An' the chance to get rid of some o' me competition?'

'That's right,' I said.

'Well,' said Bassalissa. 'The way I see it, an' I *am* a sharp woman, I'd be a fool not to.' She stood up, and stuck out her hand.

'You're the boss,' I said to Katherine.

'Oh yes, so I am,' she said, getting up and shaking Bassalissa's hand. 'Congratulations, Mrs Bugg. Welcome to the team.'

CHAPTER 13
Katherine

On Saturday, James and I visited Hazelgrove again. There was just a week to the wedding. His parents were in the drawing room as before, Mrs King in her black dress embroidering, Mr King pacing about smoking a pipe. I noticed that Mrs King's hair looked less old-fashioned. She flushed at my scrutiny.

'Thank you so much for sending the magazines to Norah,' she said. 'Edwin thought they might be too stimulating for Evangeline, but really, when I read them I saw they were quite practical and sensible in the main, and as you can see, we are slowly coming up to date.'

'I still worry about her,' grumbled Mr King. 'Dorothea won't have it but I do believe Evangeline has a feverish light.'

'Sparkling eyes, Edwin dear,' said Mrs King. 'It's a pleasure to see. Now Katherine dear, do tell me all about the wedding plans. I do hope you're not trying to do it alone. If you'd like to borrow Cook, I'm sure that could be arranged.'

I tried to imagine Ada with her good plain cooking, me with my culinary indifference and the Kings' cook, who produced seven-course meals, working together in our tiny kitchen. I had a vision of tripe vol-au-vents and stifled the urge to giggle.

'That's so kind of you,' I said, 'but my dear friend has ordered a buffet from Fortnum's to have at her house.' Connie had insisted as her wedding present to us, and I couldn't have been more grateful.

I took a breath. 'One of the guests is the esteemed Dr Farquhar. You may have heard of his research into neurology. If you will allow Evangeline to attend and be my bridesmaid, she will be quite safe.'

The Kings exchanged glances.

'Perhaps,' said Mr King. 'I have heard of him. He's not a fool, I gather.'

'Now do tell us about life in an office,' said Mrs King. 'It must be so exciting, mixing with the lions who run the Empire.'

'Fools. All of them,' said Mr King.

I restrained myself from saying that the women were allowed almost nothing to do with the men, and that most of the men I did meet there were more like cats than lions; slinking and liable to vanish at the first sign of trouble.

'Did you ever meet Andrew Fowler?' said Mr King. 'He was a fool.'

'I think I may know the name,' I said. 'But I'm

afraid he is not with us any longer.'

'Oh, it was terribly sad,' said Mrs King. 'It's true. He was taken ill and fell under a . . . what do they call them in the vernacular? *Tube train.* I must say I've never ventured underground, but I am sure looking down those tunnels must disorientate one, even if one is quite well.'

'Exactly my point. He shouldn't have attempted it while feverish,' said Mr King.

'Yes, it was quite foolish,' I agreed.

'Well, it was typical of the man. We knew him from a boy, didn't we Dorothea? One of the rector's sons. Not the current rector of course. Too many children. Andrew's father that is, not the current rector. Andrew was the cleverest.'

'I thought you said he was a fool?' said James.

'There's a distinct difference between cleverness and intelligence, James.'

'Oh, but he did so well for a man with so little means,' said Mrs King. 'He secured a good position in the Department and got on quite quickly.'

'But then he married that woman.'

'Well, yes. But I do rather think his mother put him up to it.' Mrs King turned to me. 'She was at least fifteen years older. The wife, that is. Some sort of relation, I think, with two grown children. When I say grown, the girl was seventeen and had been married off in a suspicious hurry if you get my drift, with an enormous 'premature' baby six months later. The boy was at Oxford and misbehaved repeatedly until he was sent down. Brawling, drunkenness, loose women…'

'How I miss those days,' sighed James, with a twinkle.

'James!' scolded his mother. 'Don't tease poor Katherine. If anything we were worried you were being too serious, what with your debating and your politics. We were quite unsure what you'd do. I suppose journalism is not as bad as it might have been.'

'Well, when he's bored of journalism I'm sure James will want to come back and manage the estate,' said Mr King. It seemed more of a prayer than a statement.

'What happened to the boy, Mr King?' I asked.

'Who? Oh, the lad. Somehow Fowler got him a junior position in the Department. I doubt he was or is very satisfactory. And then of course the wife died.'

'You're making it all so confusing, dear,' said Mrs King. 'When his wife died, Andrew washed his hands of her children and he seemed quite happy for a while. But then his mother, the old rector's wife, grew very concerned that he had become embroiled in spiritualism. It made him quite ill, she said.'

'Fool.'

'And it was so strange as he was doing so well. He had obtained a promotion. And yet he was so unhappy. Haunted, someone said. Very strange. And then, of course, he died. Such a shame. Never really had the chance of happiness.'

***

'Good morning, ladies.'

Mr Maynard appeared through the door in the

panelling on Monday and made us jump. I slid off my desk and tried to look as if I were in charge. Connie typed another word out of sheer nervousness. Only Mina sat unruffled, as if men appearing from walls happened all the time.

'How is the coded message coming along, Miss Swift?' He leaned over Connie's shoulder. 'I do so look forward to reading it every day.'

Connie choked on her biscuit.

'And Miss Demeray, how are things progressing? I suppose a resolution to our problem before your wedding is unlikely.'

'I'm afraid so, sir. But we do have further information. We have eliminated Aelfrida from our enquiries for…'

'Sheer incompetence,' said Mina.

'And we've ruled Bassalissa, or rather Ernestine Bugg, out. She is genuine.'

'A genuine fortune-teller? You surprise me, Miss Demeray. Please tell me they haven't hoodwinked you.'

'No,' I said. 'She can read people, that's the truth, but it's wisdom, not trickery. We . . . *I* have recruited her to this team. Naturally, we need your approval before we can admit her to the building. However, she is preparing a report this morning on strange things she's encountered since she began to, um, dabble.'

'I hope it's easier to read than Miss Swift's.' Mr Maynard paced, frowning, his hands clenched behind him. 'You will have to convince me about this woman. Have you found nothing else?'

I glanced at Mina. She gave a tiny nod. 'There's been mention of someone who worked in the Department. He had a connection with spiritualists. Lilias Cadwalader, at least.'

Mr Maynard stopped pacing. His frown grew deeper. After a while he said almost to himself, 'I thought so. I thought so.' He raised his voice. 'I don't suppose you have a name?'

'Andrew Fowler,' said Mina.

Mr Maynard was very still. 'Fowler. That's interesting. He was so very respected and then he became unreliable. There was a suspicion of opium, but I think that was just scandal-mongering. He went a little off his head, I think. Lost reports. Kept harrying people, trying to get them to meet, but wouldn't commit anything to paper. You can't get anything done in the Department without everything in triplicate, can you Miss Swift? But he's dead. And you know how it is here, when someone leaves unexpectedly, there's a flurry of excitement and then it's as if they never existed. Few would remember him now.'

'I remember typing his name,' I said.

'He was the originator of a piece of work which is still ongoing. Although some of his research is missing. Perhaps they should get a woman to do the filing, eh, Miss Swift. Are you sure it's relevant?'

I shook my head. 'I . . . don't know.'

Mr Maynard took my typed report, added another letter to Connie's sheet of paper, and left the room.

'You didn't ask about the stepson,' said Connie.

'I don't know his name. Anyway, time to get your coat. We've a matinee to attend.'

***

Even on a Monday afternoon, the theatre was full. The Sphinx had a mostly female audience, generally of the bored, monied class. Connie and Albert fitted in very well.

'James can't attend,' I said, 'but there are five of us and it's three o'clock in the afternoon.'

'I'd like to see him mind-read me,' muttered Ernestine.

'Or indeed me,' said Mina. She was pale, but her normal calm was intact. If she'd wiped a tear during the journey, Connie and I had been sure to look the other way.

'It'll be interesting,' said Albert. 'I've never seen one of these charlatans in action. Look at all these women. Agog to hear lies from a mountebank. And they want the vote. *Ouch,* K!' He rubbed his foot and shrank back in his chair. 'It was a joke, ladies, a joke. I hope you're out of practice in the ju-jitsu, K.'

'No. I'm primed and ready.'

'Shhh,' the woman in front hissed, turning. I recognised Geraldine Timpson. She narrowed her eyes.

'Aren't you the little ninny I saw out with James King a while ago? I hope you took my advice and found out a little more about him.'

'Yes, thank you, I did.' I removed my left glove to reveal the pretty engagement ring.

Mrs Timpson opened her mouth to say something,

but it was lost in a drum roll. She gave me a pitying smirk and faced forward.

'Ladies and gentlemen!' called a compère. 'Pray silence!'

The auditorium hushed.

The lights lowered and soft music began to play, though no musicians were visible. It had a steady beat like a dance tune, slightly out of kilter with my heart. A deep voice echoed round the room, bouncing from corner to corner.

'The Sphinx . . . the Sphinx . . . the Sphinx... Your thoughts are his.'

'*Ventriloquiz*,' whispered Connie.

People around us tutted and shushed.

Lights illuminated a tiny part of the stage. A man was seated, his elbows on the chair arms, studying the audience over steepled fingers. A voice, low yet distinct, spoke. 'An engagement ring, a wedding planned, a troubled young woman.' It was impossible to pinpoint the source of the voice, even knowing it came from the figure on stage. He stood and scanned the auditorium. His eyes swept over me, and back. I felt myself fighting not to stand; it was like being in a classroom when you've done something wrong, and you're trying to avoid the teacher's eye.

But it was Geraldine who stood.

'Here I am,' she said.

CHAPTER 14
Connie

I nudged Katherine and pointed at the slim form of the woman standing in the row in front. 'Do you know her?'

'Sshh, Connie,' hissed Katherine, her eyes fixed on the woman's back.

'But she —'

'*Please*,' Katherine whispered.

The Sphinx's pale eyes rested on the woman like a fly on a piece of cake. 'Here you are,' he said, urbanely. Suddenly he frowned, and placed his fingers to his temples, and his gaze seemed to intensify. 'And yet, you are not.'

An *Ahhh* from the audience.

'I sense that, in one way, you are not the person I seek. Not the person whose thoughts wheel and flutter like a bird trying to escape from its cage.'

'Ooh, he's good,' murmured Ernestine.

'And yet in another way, you are…'

Ernestine nudged me. ''Ere we go,' she said, settling in her chair as if we were watching a play. She grinned at the volley of shushes from all sides.

'You are a young woman who feels she has escaped from something . . . I cannot see what because your mind has tried to shut it away. It appals you. It disgusts you so much that you cannot bear to think about it.'

'Yes,' whispered the woman, her shoulders twitching in a way that suggested she was wringing her hands.

'Is that right? I cannot quite hear you.'

'*Yes*.' She put her hands over her mouth.

'You thought it was gone, all gone, but something . . . or someone . . . has brought it back into your mind.'

Gasps from the audience, and murmurs.

'Am I right?'

She swallowed.

'Tell me, my dear. Tell the Sphinx.'

I felt Katherine shifting in her seat beside me. 'If she even *thinks* about it —'

'You are right. It was —'

Katherine half-rose, and as she did the Sphinx held up a hand. 'You do not need to tell me what I already know.'

She sank into her seat, and I reached for her hand. It was hot and clammy. 'Do you want to leave?' I whispered, my eyes still on the woman's back.

'No,' Katherine muttered. 'I want to hear what he says. And if that woman says *anything*...'

The Sphinx removed his hands from his temples and stretched them out to the lone woman, who trembled like a leaf. 'Let me connect with you further, my child. So far I have only penetrated to a superficial level of your brain. Let me see more.'

'Yes. Yes.' The woman sounded as if she was in some sort of ecstasy.

'Reach towards me.'

She raised her arms, leaning forward slightly.

'Turn your palms upward…'

She did as she was told.

'Ah yes, that is better.' The Sphinx's long, pale fingers seemed to glow in the limelight. '*Now* I see.'

'What do you see?'

'I see a woman who ought to be happy, but she is not. Because something is — missing.'

'Ahhhh!' Her cry was one of pain, as if someone had jabbed a sharp needle into her heart.

'It is not a question of money. It is a question of — family…'

She nodded convulsively.

'Try to stay as still as you can, my dear, or you will break our connection.' Suddenly the Sphinx looked down, and his shoulders slumped.

An *Ohh* of disappointment rippled through the audience like a wave.

The Sphinx's hands returned to his temples. 'Wait. I have it. Yes. I see the problem, and I know how you can solve it.' The woman's hands were still stretched out to him, as if she were drowning and he her last hope of rescue.

'Tell me!' she cried. 'Please, tell me!'

A slow smile curled the Sphinx's thin mouth. 'I cannot tell you in front of all these people. It must be a secret between you and me. But if you ask for me when the performance is concluded, I shall speak to you alone then.'

'I bet 'e will,' said Ernestine, chuckling to herself.

'You may sit now,' intoned the Sphinx.

The woman collapsed into her chair and began to cry quietly, while her companions soothed her.

'And yet we are not done.' The pale eyes scanned the audience. 'An engagement ring, and a young woman whose mind is in turmoil.'

Katherine turned to me with anguish in her eyes. '*Help me*,' she whispered. 'Whatever he says, don't let me stand up.'

I gripped her hand tighter than ever, then leaned across her. '*Albert*,' I whispered.

He jumped, and raised his eyebrows at me.

'Take Katherine's other hand.' I looked at him. 'Don't ask why, just do it. Don't let her get up, whatever you do.'

His hand enfolded Katherine's.

'I do not think she is far from me . . . oh, her thoughts are trying to hide, but I can see them. I can see them as clear as day.'

Katherine's hand trembled in mine.

'She is frightened, unsure…'

'*No*. No I'm not.'

'Is she doing the right thing…?'

The woman in front of us turned again. 'Are you?'

She smiled. 'I think we should ask.'

'If you so much as —' hissed Katherine.

'Is she...?'

Katherine's hand began to jerk about. She wrenched it from my grip and tried to prise Albert's fingers away. And just as I thought she might succeed, Ernestine stood up and said, very calmly, 'It is I. I am the one you seek.'

***

We left the show at the interval and Albert directed Tredwell to take us to Regent's Park. 'I think we need to clear our heads with a walk,' he said.

We all looked at Katherine. She was as pale as death, apart from her freckles, and looked as if a strong wind could have blown her over. 'I'm fine,' she said.

'No you're not, K. I'm not delivering you back to James in that state.'

'For heaven's sake, Albert, I'm not a parcel. Can't you talk to me as if I had a brain?' she retorted.

'Well, this is nice,' said Ernestine, grinning. 'I thought it was the couples what 'ad the tiffs.'

'As *someone* separated me from my husband during the show,' I said, wanting to glare at Katherine but not having the heart, 'I haven't had the chance.'

'What did you make of it, Ernestine?' Mina asked.

'Load of claptrap,' said Ernestine, cheerfully. 'Nothin' I ain't seen before.'

'So you didn't feel anything when you were standing up?' Katherine asked.

'Not a thing.'

'Not even when he was really concentrating on you?' Her voice had a hint of accusation in it. 'You looked very dreamy, you know.'

'Nope.' Ernestine shook her head. 'D'you want to know what I was thinking of, when he was telling me about my troubled engagement and a stormy path and how I could calm the waters?'

'Go on,' I said.

'Sausage an' mash. A big plate, with gravy an' onions an' all.'

'That does sound nice…' I felt myself drifting off a little.

'The thing is, Miss D,' said Ernestine, 'you're young and a little what I'd call suggestible. You too, Mrs L. You've both got imagination in spades. That ain't a bad thing, except when you're dealing with a twisty bird like Professor Vitruvius.'

'She's right, you know,' said Mina.

'Although you weren't anything like as bad as her in front of us.' Ernestine stretched her arms out like a sleepwalker. 'Now her I felt proper sorry for.'

'I didn't,' snapped Katherine.

'So you do know her,' I said.

'We've never been formally introduced,' she said shortly. 'And no, I'm not going to tell you about it.' She stalked along with her head held high for a few moments. 'Why did you feel sorry for her, Ernestine?' The look on Katherine's face suggested she was hoping for something grisly.

'That weren't her first time,' said Ernestine. 'Not by a

long chalk. He reeled her in like a fish, so 'e did, and she fell for it hook, line and sinker. I thought she was a plant at first.'

'A what?' I asked.

'*You* know. One of them fake people 'oo are set up in the audience to win the crowd over. But them were real tears, I'd swear it.'

'What do you think her problem was?' Albert asked, frowning.

'She was married, that's for sure, cos I saw the ring, so I'd say from that pleading look that it's to do with a child. An' from the way she stretched her hands out when the Prof said he could solve the problem, it's that she wants a child and can't 'ave one.' Ernestine sighed. 'The Prof's probably sold her a whole ton of purifying stones and amulets and whatnot, and he'll keep her strung along till she gets lucky. Or runs out of cash.'

I shuddered, and Albert squeezed my arm. 'So . . . have you ever seen one of these acts where you couldn't work out how it was done?' I asked, to take my mind off Katherine's stormy face, and how close Albert was.

'Been giving that some thought.' Ernestine rummaged in her bag, bringing out a dog-eared mass of notepaper covered in a looping scrawl. 'I went to a good few shows when I was starting, you see, to get the lie of the land. Most of 'em was good entertainment if you kept yer brain switched off, so to speak. A few of 'em was quite convincing. I saw the Sphinx back in the day, and I must admit, 'e 'ad me fooled for a bit. 'E's got a bit of the old mesmerism goin', you see, as well as the cold reading. But what you saw jus' now is pretty much the same thing I saw five years ago. There's something twisted going on, just not as bad as some.'

'As who?' asked Mina.

Ernestine considered, and her next words came slowly. 'There was one. I don't know if it's helpers, or wires, or luck, but I couldn't see how she did it.' She paused, and swallowed. 'It was a seance, and there was ten of us in a little room. Ten punters, and her. An' she told me things about my Mr Bugg that I don't see how she could have known.'

'You don't have to tell us,' said Katherine, softly.

Ernestine's jaw clenched. 'I don't believe in spirits, nor in ghosts,' she said firmly. 'Never have, never will. But when I came out of that room, I nearly did. An' I wouldn't be alone for one minute with Lilias Cadwalader, not for all the tea in China.'

Chapter 15
Katherine

'I hope you're not worrying about what will happen while you're away on honeymoon,' said Margaret at breakfast.

I blinked, caught Mina's sardonic eye and choked on my toast. Margaret, fortunately, was too busy delving for the last of the marmalade to notice.

'We shall be fine left alone,' she continued. 'Miss Robson has arranged to hold her women's suffrage meetings here, and I shall invite all my friends. We shall raid the larder for Ada's stash of cooking brandy, then we shall denounce men and declare war on moustaches.'

The twinkle in her eye made me laugh. I half-hoped that they would.

'I can see you getting up to all sorts of shenanigans when you go to university in September,' I said. I was still a little envious, but mostly I was proud that she was not only able to, but wanted to take up an opportunity that had been denied me.

'If it wasn't for you and Connie "gallivanting" regardless of what everyone else says, I wouldn't want to go,' she said. 'I'd have carried on waiting for a man to rescue me. It never occurred to me that I could rescue the man. It won't be the same when you're married and I don't have to interrupt any shenanigans. It's been such fun.' She grinned.

'Well,' I said, grinning back, 'when you have a young man of your own, I shall repay like for like.'

'Who needs a man? Maybe I'll be proud and independent like Miss Robson.'

'Do you want to be?'

Margaret shrugged. I suspected she thought it unlikely that she would be single for long. She rose and gave me an unexpected hug.

'Oh Kitty, I'm so glad you're not getting married in secret like Connie,' she said. 'I'll help you make it the most wonderful wedding, I promise.'

The letterbox rattled and Margaret looked up.

'Nothing's likely to be so important it's worth trying to get to it before Ada,' said Mina. 'She'll bowl you over.'

Sure enough, seconds later Ada burst through the dining-room door waving the post. Her mouth was working but nothing was coming out.

'Ada! Are you all right? Sit down.'

Ada shook her head and handed me the letter.

'What is it?' said Margaret. 'Is it James? What's wrong?'

The envelope was grubby and torn in one corner. The stamp was foreign, the writing almost illegible, ink-blotted, but…

'It's from Father.'

My ears filled with humming, the edges of the world grew darker and darker, the room closed in, there was utter silence…

…the light and sound rushed back. The floor seemed very comfortable but the tablecloth was hanging unevenly. I wasn't entirely sure who or where I was.

'Steady now Miss Kitty, sit up, take a sip of tea, you'll be all right in a moment. Did you bang your head? Sit up, let me see.'

'Kitty, Kitty, sit up.'

'Let's get you on a chair, Katherine.'

I let Mina and Ada lift me off the floor. The letter was still clasped in my hand. I glanced up at Margaret. Her face was white, tiny freckles showing across her nose. I reached out for her.

'I'll make fresh tea,' said Ada.

'I'll help you, Ada,' said Mina.

Margaret and I stared at each other, then she pulled her chair next to mine and handed me a clean knife. The envelope paper was so poor that I could have slit it with a fingernail. The paper inside was covered in Father's scrawl.

'When…?'

'Six months ago,' I said. I had thought him dead. Six months ago, I had all but given up hope. A few weeks ago, I had decided to stop hoping.

'What does he say?' asked Margaret. There was a sob in her voice. 'I can't remember how to read his writing.'

I started to read aloud.

***

An hour later I was walking in the park by the office again. I was in a daze. I don't know how I got there. All I knew was that I couldn't stay at home with my thoughts a moment longer. One moment an orphan, the next back in half-orphaned limbo. I hoped Connie would arrive soon, and yet I also hoped she would be delayed. Father's words, written from somewhere called what looked like Konia, rolled round and round my head.

'*My dear Katherine and Margaret, I hope this finds you well,*' he had written, as if he'd popped away for a weekend. '*Margaret, I hope you are behaving yourself and doing as Katherine tells you. You must be quite grown up now.*'

'I'm eighteen,' Margaret had said. 'He seems to think I'm six.'

'He never knew — knows how old we are.'

'Still.'

'*It is very beautiful here and perhaps one day you might visit, although it is perhaps not quite the place for a lady at present. As you know from my previous letters…*'

'Previous letters?'

'*… there are rumblings from the two empires…*'

'Which two?'

'The Ottomans and the Greeks, I think.'

'*...which have made our time in the wilds outside Constantinople rather, shall we say, alarming. The food however is superb, and the setting sun over the olive groves as one's feet crush wild thyme and the shepherds sing and the shy maidens glimpse from behind their veils is like nectar to the soul.*'

'Which empire is he referring to?'

'I don't know. Possibly both.'

'*Katherine, I do have some terrible news for you. I hope that in the circumstances you will not be too distressed. Henry did assure me that there was no promise between you; however you must have had quite a shock when I wrote that he had married a local woman.*'

I paused.

'Oh Kitty, did he write?'

'He may have. It never arrived. It doesn't matter.'

Whatever feelings I had ever had for Henry had long gone, but a tiny part of me still felt hurt that he had married before me.

'*I know that even if there was no understanding, you were nonetheless fond of him, and you will be sad to hear that he and his bride have been killed in one of the earth tremors for which this area is known. We were all the "family" he had, and therefore we are the only ones who will mourn him. He was a wonderful secretary and I miss his company and dare I say it, his common sense. Without him, I am a little lost in a sea of current affairs which are a mystery to me, for there is a heaviness in the air which no amount of crushed thyme can sweeten and a thirst for blood which I fear could intoxicate and poison if unchecked. One should feel thrilled at the sight of a well-trained and well-armed military but somehow I feel it foreshadows great distress.*

My dear girls, I am confident you have managed our little home very well in my absence and hope that you look forward to the return of your dear Papa. I confess I am rather weary of foreign climes and remain uneasy. I look forward to publishing my research into tulips and my experiences in these troubled parts, therefore I anticipate returning in the summer of '92 or perhaps the autumn, provided nothing escalates further to prohibit my travel. I am sure there is no urgent need for my earlier return.

With much love, Father.'

Now I wandered the little paths of the quiet park as if I were the one intoxicated and poisoned. James was still at work, and all I could do was post a letter to his flat and hope that it would arrive by the afternoon post and then that he was not late home. All I wanted was his strong arms around me, his lovely chest to press my face against, his hand stroking my hair, and him telling me that everything would be all right. 'He won't be home for our wedding,' he'd say, 'but he will be home.' He'd say it even if there was still no certainty, even if the latest news from the eastern Mediterranean was not good. I almost wished I had the brainless clatter of the typing room to go to, so that I could blot it out. And poor Henry. I pictured him under rubble, trying to protect his foreign bride, and it was impossible for my eyes not to fill with tears.

I think that's why I was caught off guard. And perhaps I really had banged my head when I fainted at the breakfast table. I sensed someone rushing down the path behind me but paid no heed. My mind was whirling with doubts. Should I postpone the wedding so that Father could be there? Should I ask Uncle Maurice to see if the Foreign Office could help extract him? What if, after all, it was a false hope, and Father had not survived the earth tremors and political unrest?

The pattering footsteps slowed just as Connie's clear voice called my name.

I started to turn but it was too late. Someone was pulling on my bag. I kicked out backwards, but hampered by my skirt, I overbalanced. As I fell I sensed my assailant reaching for me. My brain took over and recalled the ju-jitsu that James had taught me. Twisting and altering my stance, with every ounce of my energy I threw the man holding me. As he toppled, his grip loosened and I jumped away.

'Here, you! Leave her alone!' Voices shouted across the park. More footsteps. The man picked himself up and rushed off as two men ran up. One took chase, while another steadied me. Connie flung her arms around me.

'Call the police!' shouted the man beside me. 'He assaulted a lady in broad daylight!'

'He's gone!' said the other, panting as he returned. 'Like a hare. Couldn't keep up. Are you all right, Miss?

Did he take anything? I can't believe it. He didn't look like a ruffian. Did you know him, Miss?'

I shook my head. 'I didn't even see his face. I don't know why —'

Connie shushed me. 'She's my friend, I'll look after her,' she said. 'I don't know what the world is coming to when a lady can't walk in St James's Park at eleven in the morning without being attacked.' She steered me down the path.

'It was that man,' she said.

'What man?' I was trembling. I didn't know whether to wish she'd stop talking nonsense, or wish it wasn't unladylike to lie on the grass and wait for everything to go away.

'The man with the pipe. The one who was listening in that day we were here with Mina.'

I tried to recall. It had only been a few days ago but the face was blurry. An average face. An office gent.

'Connie,' I said, my voice shaking, 'this is all too much. I don't want to do this any more. I just want to get married. I just want to get married and be a housewife and have my father home, and for the biggest of my worries to be whether James will like what I've ordered for dinner. I just want to get married and be ordinary so much.'

'Shh,' said Connie. It felt as if the world was upside down. She was steering me along a side street, towards a small coffee-shop. It was full of smoke and men, all of whom turned to look at us, decided we were of no interest, and returned to their conversations.

'Sit down,' she said. 'There are no old cats to listen in, and some coffee will do you good. Brandy would be better, but I daresay one of Mother's friends would spot us if we went to a public house, and it's too complicated to explain. One thing at a time. Did he hurt you?'

I rubbed my arms. 'Not really.'

'Did he take anything?'

'I don't think so. There wasn't time.'

Connie looked askance. 'Aren't you going to check?'

I pulled my bag onto my lap and opened it. My purse was inside, with a notebook and pencil, a copy of *Three Men in a Boat*, and a photograph of James. And an envelope.

'Oh Katherine. Is that the letter from your father, the one you sent the wire about?'

'No.' I rummaged in my bag again. Father's letter was gone, or . . . hadn't I left it at home? I pulled out the envelope. It was addressed in typescript to Miss 'Caster'. Exactly like that. Inside was a letter, addressed to me.

Miss Demeray. You have worked in the Department for some time. You know that it is Wicked that Secrets are suppressed which could Overturn Empires and let the Righteous Flourish. Share them and your loyalty to Justice will be rewarded. If you do not believe, listen to the spirits. Andrew Fowler did not understand what they were trying to communicate. Trust us. A Friend.

Chapter 16
Connie

Katherine passed me the letter and I reread it. '*A Friend*', I repeated. 'I doubt that very much. What sort of friend tries to attack you in broad daylight?'

'One that knows who I am.' Katherine sounded dazed. 'How?'

'I don't know. But this has to be stopped. That I do know.' I drained my coffee cup. 'Come on, we're going to the office.'

'But it isn't an office day.'

'No, but we need to talk about this properly in a place where we feel safe.'

Katherine nodded, putting the letter away. She was quiet on the short walk to the office, holding her bag tight. It was only when we reached our floor, and I locked the door behind us, that she seemed to breathe at all.

'Do you think it's safe to leave Margaret alone?' she

asked. 'What if I go on honeymoon and something happens?'

'I don't think it will,' I said. 'They're not interested in Margaret. It's you they want, and your secrets. Sorry, *Secrets.*'

A smile flickered on Katherine's lips. 'The writer does seem addicted to capital letters,' she observed. 'It's like a political pamphlet, or a religious tract.' She took the letter from her bag again, and we pored over it.

'Entirely typewritten, so there's no handwriting to trace,' I commented.

'And no name or instructions on how to meet, either,' said Katherine. 'Presumably he'll find me. He's good at that. I might study my self-defence book tonight.'

'But who is it, and what do they want?' I tapped the paper. '*Secrets are suppressed which could Overturn Empires . . . Share them.*'

'He knows I worked here before,' said Katherine, frowning. 'I wonder…'

'What do you wonder?'

'Come and sit with me,' she said suddenly, taking my hand and leading me to a chair. She fetched another and placed it beside mine. 'Imagine you're the letter-writer.'

I wrinkled my nose. 'I'd rather not.'

'Very well. *I'm* the letter-writer. I work in the Department — bear with me, Connie — and I've seen the various women in the typing room going in and out, in and out for years. One of them, a small red-haired one, disappears. I probably assume she's left to get married. Then she reappears some months later, but not in the typing room. She's in a room upstairs, with a different manager, and no-one knows quite what she or the other women in her section do.'

'Isn't the official line something about paranormalists and tax?' I said.

'It is, but why would they get women to work on that? Surely they'd just send letters. He's on to us, for sure.'

'But why does he care what you're doing? Why would it matter to him?'

'There are two options. Either he thinks I'm doing more than investigating paranormalists, and he wants to know what it is. Or else it's simply that he wants me to stop. He doesn't want us to report anything bad about them.' Katherine shivered. 'He was hanging around outside Aelfrida's when we visited. He was loitering in the park when we went for a walk. And he was there just now. That's either an awful lot of coincidences, or he's been spying on us pretty much since we started work.'

'But who *is* he?'

'He's nondescript, he's dressed like a clerk…' Katherine's voice trailed off, and she gazed into nothingness.

'It isn't much to go on, I know,' I sympathised.

Katherine did not reply.

'I mean, there must be a hundred men who fit that description. A thousand, even.'

Still no response. Katherine looked as if she were trying to work out a long-division sum in her head.

'How many men work at the Department, anyw —'

'*Connie.*' Katherine rounded on me. 'Please be quiet for a moment.'

'I'm sorry,' I said, feeling rather injured. 'I was just pursuing a line of enquiry.'

'You can stop now. I know who he is.' Her eyes sparkled for the first time in an age. 'Don't you see?'

'I might, if someone would share *their* secrets.'

'There's only one person in the world he could be. He's Andrew Fowler's stepson.'

***

'Now I see,' I said. 'Share secrets, and you'll be rewarded. Is that what Andrew Fowler did?'

'Possibly.' Katherine sighed. 'How am I going to tell Mina?'

'You can't tell her anything till you're sure, that's for certain.' I got up and began to pace. 'I still don't see how it all fits together. Has the stepson been sharing Department information, too? Which section does he work in?'

'There's something else, too,' said Katherine, almost running to meet me. '*Listen to the spirits*. The people we've been investigating are part of this — they must be! Lilias Cadwalader most of all, since she was the one Andrew consulted.'

'Would Mina know the stepson's name?'

'If she does, we could ask Mr Maynard where he works, or Reg even. Reg knows everyone —' Katherine stopped, and seemed to shrink a little. 'But I probably won't be here for any of that,' she said, flatly.

'Well, no. Not unless we put our investigation on hold for the week.'

'Why does everything have to happen at once?' Katherine wailed. 'News about Father, and all this, *and* getting married?'

I put my hands on her shoulders. 'Calm down, Katherine. From what you've told me about your father, he'll come home when he's ready, and not a moment before. Andrew Fowler's been dead for ten years, so he can wait another week. You can't chase Mystery Man; he wants to come to you. The only thing you can't put off is getting married, and why would you want to?'

'I don't want to,' Katherine said, in a slightly sulky voice. 'Not at all.'

'Good. We can't un-order the flowers now, you know.'

'I suppose.' She brightened a little. 'Perhaps when I come back I could write to Lilias Cadwalader yet again for an appointment.'

'Yes, you could. Perhaps you might even get to see her before the end of the year.'

'But what *will* happen here while we're on our honeymoon?' Katherine gazed round the quiet room as if she expected it to be full of frenetic activity.

'I'll be in charge,' I said slowly. 'That's all you need to know.'

***

When I got home, Johnson informed me that Albert was in the study. 'He's been in there a while, ma'am.'

This made me quail a little; but then I rallied. I had

news which he would want to know. 'Thank you, Johnson. Has he had lunch?'

'Not yet, ma'am.'

'Then I shall go and see if he wants some.'

I knocked, and an abstracted voice called 'Come!' An abstracted voice, not an angry one. I could have sighed with relief.

I had half-expected Albert to be buried in a pile of papers, but one sheet of paper lay on his desk. 'Oh!' he said, when he saw me. 'I thought you were lunching with Katherine.'

'I was, but so much has happened...' I sat down in the armchair and poured out the story of the attack, and the letter, and the small matter of the letter from Katherine's father. 'I did offer her lunch, but she wasn't hungry. I think she's in shock, a little. She said she'd rather go home, so I dropped her on the way back.'

'I'm not surprised.' A wry smile. 'I've been busy, too.'

My eyes flicked to the sheet of notepaper on his desk. 'What have you been doing?'

'Composing increasingly rude replies to this letter.' He sighed. 'I've kept them in my head, so far, since if I actually sent one of them Father would probably never speak to me again.'

'What is it this time?'

Albert slid the letter across the desk. 'Read it if you like. The gist is that he wants to take control of his money.'

My eyes scanned the letter. '...*control of the estate to*

revert to me immediately . . . dribs and drabs of money . . . no way to manage investments . . . unnecessarily secretive...' I couldn't bear to read any more. While Albert's wry smile remained, it was that of a man who is determined not to show that his enemy has wounded him.

'What will you do?' I asked, pushing the letter back towards him.

Albert's hand covered mine, took it up. 'I'll cede control, if that's what he wants. Of course I shall. It's his money, not mine. But there's one thing I must do first.' A little spark of mischief danced in his eyes. 'I must let my brother Maurice know the arrangements to date. As he is the eldest son, and stands to inherit, I think that's only fair.'

'Oooh.' I had met Maurice Lamont junior briefly at our wedding; a tall, dark, languid man who lived, if I recalled correctly, in rooms somewhere unfashionable. 'When will you do that?'

'Well,' Albert said, turning the letter over, 'this came by the mid-morning post, not long after you left. I composed a fairly hasty letter to Maurice, and sent Johnson to the post-office with it about an hour ago. So the ball is in Maurice's court. Assuming he deigns to open the letter and read it.' His voice was light, offhand.

'You don't — mind — that he'll know about your investments?'

Albert shrugged. 'It's a family matter, and it's important. I've asked him to keep it to himself, certainly for now. If he needs proof, he can meet with Anstruther.

Anyway...' He stretched out in his chair. 'We both deserve lunch, and you in particular. I wouldn't want to be in charge of a government section.'

'It's two other people, for three days. Don't forget you have additional responsibilities, too.'

Albert grimaced in mock-horror. 'Don't remind me. Rings to keep safe, ushers to brief, speech to write, groom to deliver...'

'There. Unmasking a government conspiracy will be nothing in comparison.'

'True.' Albert got up, leaned over the armchair, and kissed me. 'As we are both very important people in charge of weighty matters, we need a lunch of equivalent proportions. While Mrs Jones's cooking has improved, I feel an outing to Simpson's would be more fitting to our requirements. Would you agree, Connie?'

'Motion carried,' I murmured, and kissed him back.

CHAPTER 17
Katherine

On Wednesday I pulled myself together and went into work. Mina said little as we hurried breakfast then swayed in the tube train, although she did, I noticed, appear to take notes while reading Father's letter. It had been safe, placed in the study with his only other letter. All the ones which had never reached us hovered in my thoughts. Would they have made the delay more clear? Or his location? Was he more at risk from earthquakes than militia, or was there another threat?

On the underground another thought struck me. 'You don't suppose Father has married too?'

'It's a possibility,' said Mina. I bridled for a second, expecting platitudes, and then remembered that Mina's greatest quality was that she never gave them. 'I didn't know your father terribly well,' she continued. 'I met him just a few times, when I visited Alice here before his departure. As you probably remember, he made himself scarce in the presence of women who asked questions.'

She was right, of course. Father had all the time in the world for women like Thirza Gregory, who had hung off his every word as his tales grew wilder and less likely. Women like Mina tended to demand evidence.

Mina mused. 'Alice said he was quite lost when your mother died. I didn't get the impression that he was interested in marrying again. I shouldn't worry. I'm sure that had he done so, there would have been mention of it in the latest letter, even in passing.'

'Do you think…' I shook myself. We had been over this a hundred times; me, Margaret, Mina, Connie, James. There was no way of telling whether he was still alive; we just had to carry on as before. Or almost as before. At least now we had a location. 'James has —'

'Yes, I'm sure.' Mina nudged me into silence. 'Let's get off and walk the rest of the way.'

It wasn't our stop, but she marshalled me onto the pavement anyway.

'It's far nicer to be in the open air,' she said. I glanced at the clouds which, in typical April fashion, were making up their mind whether to empty or disperse. We hadn't an umbrella. I hurried in her wake and we just reached the office steps as the first drops fell, twinkling in confused sunshine and creating a vague rainbow above us.

'If I believed in omens,' said Mina, 'I would feel very cheered. Come along, they'll be waiting.'

'They? Has Mr Maynard given Ernestine clearance?'

'I don't think so.'

We pattered up the spiral staircase, passed a group of smirking men on the landing and entered our room. For the first time I noticed how completely any sound was shut out. Within, dressed in a smart suit, leaning over Connie's shoulder, and adding to her missive with a force which threatened to bend the keys, was Reg.

'Wotcher,' he said. 'Or should I say . . . good morning, ladies.' He made a small bow, then rubbed his jaw. 'How d'yer talk like that all the time? Makes yer face ache.'

'Hullo, Reg,' I said. 'Are you allowed in here?' In the short time since I'd last seen him he'd shot up in height, and it was possible to see the young man he would become. A thin layer of fuzz was visible on his upper lip.

'Special dispensary or somefink, I mean something. Can't believe you've left me off of the team this long. But I'm prepared to let bygones be bygones.'

'That's wonderful, but —'

'After she brought you home yesterday Miss F, I mean Mrs L, had a brainwave.'

Connie sat up straight and pulled a face which I think she meant to express intelligence, but actually made her look as if she had indigestion.

'So she sent me a wire to meet her here, and we had a word with Mr Maynard,' said Mina. 'I also, I have to confess, intercepted a wire from James.'

'Addressed to me?' How could they?

'It was strictly business. And you had had enough.

We needed to bring it in so that someone, in this case Reg, could start digging.'

James had come round in the evening and sat with me in the big armchair in Father's study, holding me tight in his lap. Even Ada had left us alone, knowing that James was not the sort to take advantage of my distress. We had kissed and he had wiped my eyes. 'If you want to postpone the wedding, I'll understand,' he'd said. 'Your happiness is all I want.' I knew then that no matter what, the wedding would go ahead.

'I'm marrying you,' I'd said through my kisses, 'if I have to ju-jitsu assailants to get down the aisle, and get Mina to keep the mediums out by throwing holy water at them. And if Father turns up halfway through, he'd better not raise any objections.'

But he hadn't mentioned a wire.

I read it now. *Mother checked church register STOP A Fowler married Frances Gwinnett STOP witnesses Maximilian Gwinnett (son) Vaughan Treeves (son in law) STOP J*

'So now we know —'

'Which is where Reg came in. He's been wading through staff records from 1877.'

'Yes,' said Reg, flourishing a sheet of paper. 'Maximilian Gwinnett, employed as junior clerk on the foreign recip . . . riciprococol . . . reciprocals section.'

'What does that do?'

'Garn. No one knows what anyone does. You should know that, Miss D.'

'At a guess,' said Mina, 'trade agreements, and

decisions about managing interests abroad. More or less interesting depending on the other country, our relationship with it and current affairs.'

'I see,' said Connie. 'Is he still there?'

'The thing is,' said Reg, 'his record's not good. He's been shunted from section to section, cos he kept misfiling things, and sending documents to the wrong place. Nothing important, but they didn't like to trust him. Seems like Mr Fowler got it in the ear for putting him forward. Then the records show his mother died in 1878.'

'Yes, that's right,' said Mina.

'But is he still there?' asked Connie. 'What does he look like?'

'Now as to the first,' said Reg, 'it's a bit strange. He got suspended in '82. Something big got mislaid. Kicking screaming sorta mislaid. An' he said the thing that went missing wasn't his fault but Mr Fowler's. After Mr F kicked the bucket, Mr G was reinstated.' Mina winced, but otherwise remained impassive. 'He's still here. But I dunno what he looks like and it's not clear where he's working neither. Either.'

'And that's it,' said Connie, slumping in her chair.

'Not quite,' said Reg, 'I checked the other things you asked about. The typewriters.'

'Typewriters?' I said.

'Yes,' said Connie. 'On the letter you were sent, the lower case "t" and "m" look out of line, the same as the upper case "C" on mine.'

'So I checked all the typewriters after the ladies had

gone home,' said Reg, 'and guess what?'

'What?'

'It was typed on yours, Miss Robson.'

'Mine?' exclaimed Mina.

'Ah, young Reg!' We jumped at Mr Maynard's voice. 'Made your report?'

'Yessir, except to tell Miss D, I mean Demeray, that Ma'll look forward to seeing her in our place at six. She says it's to talk about something weddingy.'

I frowned. The last fitting had been two days ago, and the dress was in my wardrobe at home.

'Ah yes, the wedding,' said Mr Maynard. 'Day after tomorrow, isn't it? So I don't expect you or Miss Swift in tomorrow. And I hope you remember when you come back as a married woman that I'm not allowed to employ married women.'

'Yes, sir.'

'Which means you won't get a departmental gift. Now then Reg, off you go. Mr Tomlinson will be waiting for you. So, ladies, what have we discovered?'

'I'm not sure,' said Connie.

I reread James's telegram. 'Why does the name Vaughan Treeves ring a bell?' I said.

Mina ran her finger over the letters. 'I know what you mean,' she said. 'It reminds me of something, too.'

***

The following day, Connie refused to let me talk about work any further. 'Trust Mina and me,' she said. 'You need to get ready for the wedding.' She took me to lunch in the tearoom where we'd once disgraced ourselves by collapsing. The waitress looked as if she were trying to place us, but she clearly couldn't work out if we were the same people. Connie fidgeted with her teacup until I feared she would snap the handle off.

'Whatever's the matter?' I asked.

'It's . . . has anyone talked to you about...' She leaned towards me and dropped her voice, 'married life?'

'You're making it sound like a death sentence.'

'Oh no! Am I? Jemima said on no account to listen to Mother or I'd have nightmares, so I didn't. I did ask Jemima but she wasn't a lot of help.'

'Whatever are you — Oh.'

Connie wrung her hands.

I smiled. 'Don't worry, Aunt Alice explained everything when I was fifteen.'

'Aunt Alice? But, well, did she know anything?'

'Judging by what Maria told me last night, no.' I grinned. 'You seem to have survived very happily so far, Connie, and I'm sure I shall. You needn't explain anything. I really don't want to know what you are doing with, or to, my cousin.'

'Oh, what a relief,' she said, fanning herself. 'I feel quite faint. I think I should have some more cake.'

***

I felt so small next to Uncle Maurice. He looked down at me as if he'd never seen me before, and then smiled.

'You look beautiful, Katherine. I remember your parents' wedding day and you look even more lovely than your mother did. She would be very proud. I am sorry that I am a poor substitute for your father.'

I wanted to tell him it didn't matter, but I could feel my eyes filling.

'Don't cry,' said Margaret. 'When Father returns we'll show him the photographs. He wouldn't want you miserable. You can't be sad on your wedding day.'

Connie found a handkerchief and dabbed at my eyes. She leaned close. 'Your last chance, Katherine,' she whispered. 'Last chance for me to warn you about the wedding night.' Then she stepped back, grinning.

I couldn't help but laugh. 'Bet you'd be more embarrassed than I,' I muttered.

'Here's Hodgkins,' said Connie. 'Come along, Margaret.' The two of them swept down the steps arm in arm, one tall and brunette, one smaller and auburn. The soft blue of their dresses reflected the sky.

'Albert thought you'd like Tredwell to drive us,' said Uncle Maurice. 'Something about "old times' sake".'

Tredwell tipped his cap as Uncle Maurice helped me into the carriage. It seemed absurd when the church was just round the corner, but we would need it to get to Connie's later. Our wedding breakfast would be at Albert and Connie's house, in their lovely drawing room, with my going-away outfit and luggage upstairs ready for later. The sun was warm and golden. The scent of spring filled the air. We stepped into the cool of the church and there were my lovely friends and family. The Lamonts, very proud and upright, mingling happily with Aunt Alice and her husband, random country relations, and Miss Gregory, and in a more puzzled fashion with Maria, Reg and Ellen. On the other side, the Kings sat with Dr Farquhar, James's friends from work and various charities, and even Sam Webster. And stepping out from the pew to link arms with Margaret was Evangeline.

Oh Father, I thought, *you go halfway round the world to find the strange and bizarre and you could be here.*

'Are you ready?' whispered Uncle Maurice. I nodded.

We began our walk down the aisle and the two men at the altar turned. I assumed one was Albert, tall and dark, but he was just a blur.

All I could see was James.

CHAPTER 18
Connie

I felt as if my heart would burst as I walked behind Katherine, arm in arm with her sister. My best friend was getting married at last to a man only slightly less wonderful than my own husband, who was standing at his side. Memories from my own wedding less than a year before rushed back, of things that had barely registered at the time; the scent of roses, the murmurs from the congregation, and the din of the organ as I had trembled on my father's arm.

That was all I could be sad about; that Katherine's father could not be there. *At least there is hope of his return*, I told myself.

We reached the altar, and I lifted Katherine's veil. She looked so happy that a light seemed to shine out of her. I stepped back, and we three bridesmaids slipped into the nearest pew. Evangeline beamed, her eyes fixed on her brother. Margaret leaned over. 'She looks lovely, doesn't she?' she whispered, just as the organ stopped playing.

I nodded; but at that moment I heard a slight rattle at the back of the church. It came again; a metallic sound. 'Excuse me,' I murmured. I slipped out of the pew and crept down the aisle, trying not to mind everyone's eyes on me. Reg was sitting in an aisle seat a few rows behind; I caught his eye, and presently his quiet steps followed me.

A click, and the church door began to move. A latecomer? I blinked at the sudden shaft of sunlight; and when I opened my eyes, they focused on a slim, elegant shape.

The woman from Vitruvius's show, who had been rude to Katherine. The woman whom Katherine would not discuss, even with me. And her gloating expression indicated she was not there to wish the happy couple well.

I pushed the door closed and drew the bolt across. I sighed with relief, then jumped as the verger sidled up to me. 'Madam, you must leave the door open,' he muttered. 'This is a public event.'

'Very well. Carry on.' I unbolted the door, opened it, and grabbed the woman's arm as she stumbled forward. I marched her away so quickly that she almost lost her footing.

'Let go!' she cried. Reg seized her other arm, and fell into step with me. 'I'll call a policeman!'

'No you won't,' I said, coming to a halt. 'If you try, I shall tell him what you were about to do. And I shall make sure your husband knows that, and also where you were a few nights ago.'

She glared at me, panting. 'Perhaps I have reason,' she said.

'To ruin my best friend's wedding? I don't think so.'

'I was his fiancée, you know.' Her smile turned my stomach. 'Until I heard about his mad imbecile of a sister.'

I wanted to slap her. 'If you mean the person I think you do, she is behaving much better than you are right now. You ought to be ashamed of yourself.'

'I warned her, you know, but she wouldn't listen.' She struggled once more, then her arm was limp in my grasp. 'He said I should do what I thought was right,' she murmured, trying to pull away. 'I want to go home.'

'Do you have money?' I asked, and she shot me a pitying glance.

'Of course I have money.' She drew herself up. 'Get me a cab,' she said to Reg.

Reg raised his eyebrows, I nodded, and he stepped forward, arm raised. A moment later, a passing hansom slowed for us. 'Where to?'

'Chester Square,' she said. Reg opened the door for her. 'You can go now,' she told us.

'Not till we've seen you on your way,' I replied. We stood firm until the cab had rattled off in the direction of Belgravia.

''Ope we haven't missed too much, Mrs L,' said Reg, as we retraced our steps.

'I hope so too, Reg.' I sighed.

A hymn was in progress as we returned, and I slipped into my pew without too many mutterings, though I had felt eyes on my back as I hurried down the aisle. 'What were you doing?' Margaret muttered.

'Taking care of business,' I replied, hoping I looked less hot and flustered than I felt. 'Has everything been all right here?'

She looked at me as if I had taken leave of my senses. 'Of course it has,' she said witheringly.

'He's done the lawful impediment bit?'

'*Yes.*'

'Good.' I picked up my hymn book and found the right place just as the hymn finished.

I spent most of the next twenty minutes trying not to cry. I think it was a combination of the crisis I had just forestalled, memories of a year ago, and joy for my friends. 'Marriage seems to make you awfully sentimental,' Margaret whispered, disapprovingly.

'It isn't just me.' Evangeline was dabbing at her eyes too. Beyond her the Kings were whispering together, looking concerned. *If you'd seen what I had a few minutes ago*, I thought, *you'd realise how little there is to worry about.*

'With this ring I thee wed,' the priest intoned, and James echoed him. He held the ring on Katherine's finger, and when it slid to its new home, it looked as if had always been there. She glanced down at it for a moment, then at James; already, something about her was different. They knelt; the priest read a prayer; he joined their right hands; and at long last, the words 'I

161

now pronounce that they be man and wife together' rang out.

There were more prayers, more pronouncements, but I heard none of it. James and Katherine were married, and there was nothing anyone could do about it.

***

'What happened back there?' Albert murmured, as we followed Mr and Mrs King — oh, how strange and wonderful! — out of the church.

'Crisis prevention,' I murmured. 'Tell you more later.' I looked around for our intruder, but she had not returned. My joy was complete.

James and Katherine turned to us. 'We did it!' Katherine said, with a rather bemused look on her face.

'You have, K,' said Albert. 'You've gone and done it. Congratulations!'

'Well done, Mrs King,' I added. 'There, I got to say it first!'

'Katherine King,' James said, taking Katherine's hand and smiling. 'It does have a ring to it. As does this, now.' He raised her hand to his lips.

'Save something for later, you two,' Albert said briskly. 'Come along, into the carriage with you.' He shook hands with James, murmuring words that made him laugh and clap Albert on the back. James handed Katherine into the carriage, watched by a grinning Tredwell, and we waved until they had vanished.

'Could it be that the unflappable Albert Lamont is a tiny bit moved by it all?' I enquired.

'Don't know what you mean,' said Albert, blinking.

'Anyway, I must go and pay the priest.' His eyes narrowed as he looked at me. 'What *did* happen, Connie?'

People were leaving the church, trickling out in twos and threes, talking and flourishing handkerchiefs and putting on gloves and straightening bonnets, ready for the next stage. 'I can't tell you,' I said. 'I shall later, I promise. But right now we need to make sure everything runs smoothly.'

***

By a minor miracle our servants had managed to unpack the wedding breakfast and set it out without dropping it or rendering it inedible. Albert and James both kept their speeches short, safe and relatively scandal-free, and I heaved a sigh of relief that finally I could relax and enjoy myself. I caught Katherine admiring her ring at least five times, and she hardly ate a thing. 'You still need to eat once you're married,' I murmured, and popped a petit four into my mouth.

'I'm just too excited. I don't even know where we're going on honeymoon yet.'

'You'll find out soon enough.' I looked at her flushed cheeks, her sparkling eyes, and promised myself that I would not tell Katherine about the strange woman who had tried to stop the wedding, not unless I absolutely had to. And certainly not until she had returned to the office. Then my eye was caught by my tallest darkest brother-in-law, Maurice junior, approaching our table. He wore a beautifully-cut suit and apart from a flourishing moustache, slightly receding hair, and fifteen years, he could have been Albert's double.

'Hullo, Moss,' said Katherine. 'I haven't seen you since Connie and Albert's wedding.'

'Hullo Moss,' Albert murmured, wiping his mouth. He stood, and leaned over to shake his brother's hand. Maurice Lamont looked, if anything, rather wary. Albert picked up his wine glass and they retreated into a corner. Albert seemed to be doing most of the talking, with an occasional nod from his brother.

'Are they catching up?' Katherine asked.

'Something like that.'

Then I heard a muttered 'Dammit' from further along the table. Mr Lamont stood too, his chair scraping back. He drained his glass, set it down, and stomped towards Albert and Maurice. 'Having a little chat, are we?' he said as he reached them.

Albert drew himself up as he looked at his father. 'We are, yes. Just as I advised you we would.'

'Not very gentlemanly to leave your father out of things, is it?'

'What's going on?' Katherine asked, craning to see.

'Nothing. Well, something. I'll try and head it off.'

I got up and approached them. Mr Lamont was glaring at Albert. 'Make a laughing-stock of me, will you?'

'Lower your voice, Father,' said Albert, glaring back. 'This is a wedding breakfast, in case you need reminding.'

'Don't you *dare* tell me what to do, Bertie,' Mr Lamont half-shouted. Out of the corner of my eye, I saw

Katherine start.

'That is *enough!*' I snapped. I took Mr Lamont's arm and marched him along the corridor, wondering how many more times I would have to do that today. I leaned down and muttered into his ear. 'If you want to have a row, take it somewhere else. I am not having my best friend's wedding breakfast ruined by your family arguments. Either behave, or leave.'

I released his arm, and he glowered at me. His frown, his heaving chest, and his clenched teeth reminded me of a bull about to charge. Albert approached us, and while he appeared calm, his jaw was set.

Mr Lamont turned on him. 'Is this the thanks I get?' he demanded. 'I brought you up, settled money on you, and you treat me like this?'

'You were making a scene,' Albert said. 'I informed Moss, just as I said I would, and he asked to have a quiet word.'

'Maurice has no say in it!' Mr Lamont shouted. 'My house, my money, my rules!'

'And this is our house, paid for with our money, and these are our rules.' Albert looked down at him. 'Please leave, Father.'

'If you think this is the way to persuade me, you're wrong.' Mr Lamont was quiet now, but it was an ominous quiet. 'I'm going to see Anstruther first thing tomorrow. If you make any trouble, Bertie, I'll take steps.'

Albert's lip curled. 'I shall make no trouble. I leave that to you.'

We watched his father stamp and mutter his way out of the house, until the front door banged behind him. 'That went well,' murmured Albert.

'Do you think he'll actually do it?' I asked.

His mouth turned up at one corner. 'I know he'll do it.'

'Oh dear.' I looked up at him.

'It's the rest of the family I worry about,' he said. 'I mean, they're fairly comfortable, but —' That *but* hung in the air like a suspended sword.

I took his arm. 'We can't do anything now. Let's get Katherine and James sent off, and we can worry later.'

His mouth twitched. 'That sounds delightful.' And he let me steer him back into the drawing room. Maurice was hovering, but Albert shook his head and mouthed '*Another time.*'

Katherine was staring into space, running a finger round the rim of her wine glass. She jumped when I sat down beside her. 'Is everything all right?' she asked, absently.

'Everything is fine,' I said, much more confidently than I felt. 'It's almost time for your big adventure.'

James turned round. 'Did someone say adventure?' he asked, grinning. He looked at his watch, and whistled. 'It *is* time, if we're going to catch our train. Come on, Mrs King, you need to get changed.' He took Katherine's hand and pulled her to her feet.

'We're going on a train?' Katherine asked, laughing and nervous all at once.

'We might be. Now go and change!'

They reappeared — from separate rooms — fifteen minutes later, bags packed and ready. 'You'll look after everything, won't you?' Katherine murmured as I hugged her. 'The bureau, and Margaret, and —'

'Of course I shall.' I squeezed her tight. 'You just worry about James.'

'Oh, I do,' she said, with a smile. 'Thanks for all this.'

'Good luck, K,' said Albert, hugging her too. 'Keep him in line.'

'Anyone would think I was some sort of monster,' said James, rather proudly. 'Now let me carry my woman off in peace.' He scooped Katherine up and carried her to the door, amid cheers from the guests.

We watched from the doorway as James and Katherine boarded the carriage and waved from the window until they, then the carriage, were specks among the London traffic.

'Another happy ending,' said Albert, putting his arms around my waist. 'Partly thanks to you, I think.'

'Only a little bit.' I put my hand up to his cheek. 'I just hope that everything runs smoothly for the next week. No alarms, no surprises.'

Albert leaned down. 'Oh yes, of course,' he murmured into my ear. 'You're in charge, aren't you?'

I sighed. 'Don't remind me.'

CHAPTER 19
Mina

REPORT OF MISS WILHELMINA ROBSON

My dear Katherine,

I shall, naturally, present my report in a more formal manner for the official records — but felt you would appreciate the more human elements in this introduction.

I would like to explain in full what led to the events on that fateful Monday. On the one hand we seek to uncover, I am now certain, a crime of treason. On the other hand, we are embroiled in a fraud which taps into human fears and doubts at their most irrational. I am not sure which I believe is more wicked. Governments come and go, Empires rise and fall, but the human heart and soul remains ever desperate for peace.

Do not misunderstand me. I am, like your Aunt Alice and your dear mother, a good churchwoman. Not out of leave that house deserves a medal, if not a knighthood.'

'Yes,' I said, 'he is very interesting. But I wish to speak of something else. Have you any experience of mediums?'

'I confess they are not of interest to me.' Miss Bailey's voice was cold and distant. She made as if to walk away, clearly expecting me to try to persuade her.

'Nor I,' I said. 'Or at least, not from the perspective of belief or desire to believe. I would like to expose one.'

Penelope Bailey turned back. 'You interest me,' she said. 'But surely this is a matter for the police.'

'Perhaps, but they would need evidence. However, the person I would like to consult suspects me. She will not give me an audience, but she might give you one.' I held out my hand as her expression closed. 'I wish to borrow your name and undertake it myself. Miss Bailey, we barely know each other, but…'

'Has this anything to do with James teaching Katherine martial arts in my garden?'

'In a roundabout sort of way, yes.'

Miss Bailey took a glass of champagne from a passing maid and appraised me. We were the same height, of similar colouring, and while I was older, the Indian sun had aged her skin whereas heredity and a lifetime of office work and bonnets under English skies had kept mine pale and smooth. Her face changed once more; a broad mischievous grin just like James's spread over it.

'Capital,' she said at last, 'an adventure. Do call me Penelope.'

We talked where it was hard to be overhead, laughing as if it was a light, frivolous chat, until you, Katherine, departed with James. No-one seemed to follow you as you left, but there was a definite presence when I did an hour later. I had been right to be cautious.

The weekend was uneventful for us and, it appears, for the Lamonts, at least in respect of the task in hand. On Monday morning I received a wire from Penelope, and the plan was afoot.

***

I do recall being your age, Katherine. I dare say that the following will astound you, but when you are forty-seven you will understand. Age is mostly on the outside. Inside I am as much of a girl, if not more so, than Margaret. Penelope's appointment with Lilias was for seven p.m. Connie had given me the name of a reliable cabbie, Sam Webster, who picked me and a large parcel up at six. Penelope's carriage likewise collected her from Kensington.

I had borrowed Margaret's most up-to-date hat and coat as we are much the same build from a distance, and if anyone were watching, they might be less likely to follow me if they thought I were your sister. However, just to be safe, Penelope and I had planned to go right into the middle of Piccadilly, where the road was crowded and chaotic. Sam banged on the roof as soon as he was certain the persons following were lost in the throng, and somehow Sam's cab and Penelope's carriage found themselves next to each other. At that point, Penelope and I swapped places. Within the 'wrong' carriages we changed into clothes from each other's station in life, so that I arrived at Lilias's house with a false Alexandra fringe and dressed in black silk as a rich woman of middle years, wearing a thin veil, and accompanied by a maid with such level-headedness she would make Ada seem flighty.

There was nothing to link me with me, if you understand. I doubt they had paid any attention to the guest list at the wedding.

I was not the only person at the seance. There was an agitated young man whose tapping foot made me wonder how any spirit could compete. An older man and his wife were in attendance, both in deep mourning, their hands clasped, heartbreak embroidered into every line on their faces. And there was another man, youngish, louche, sitting back with a cigarette in his mouth and his arms crossed. He didn't seem to belong there at all.

We sat in silence round a low table covered in green damask, until Lilias came into the room. An ordinary woman to look at, wearing a sleeveless black dress and with her hair loose. It is hard to describe her; she was a complete 'everywoman'. Penelope's maid sat at the rear of the room, and I pitied any spirit who tried to trouble her.

The seance was, from a purely scientific point of view, fascinating. The lights were lowered and yet somehow light shone on Lilias's face. Sweet incense filled the air. There was knocking in the space above our heads, quite eclipsing the agitated boy's foot-tapping.

There were revelations.

Lilias was ashen-faced and sweat formed on her brow. 'Let the spirits speak,' she said, and a glass moved of its own accord across the tablecloth, spelling out words of love and devotion for Mama and Papa. They wept and talked of kittens and home and begged forgiveness, but the glass fell silent.

Lilias's voice changed; the deep tones of a man issued from her mouth. 'Do not worry and wealth will be yours.'

'But…' said the agitated young man.

'Do as they ask and all shall be well. Secrets are better shared. For the good of all. For the Empire.'

He slumped but his foot-tapping increased. Tears reflected in the candlelight.

Lilias turned to the nonchalant man. 'The spirits have nothing to say to you, but this does not mean there is nothing that should be said.'

She fell back in her chair and her servant approached to wipe her brow and give her water. She looked at me. It was extraordinary. I understood how you must have felt in the theatre when you are usually so unsuggestible. She was ordinary-looking but her stare was not. It was all I could do to stop myself from asking to speak to Andrew, but I did not. I did not. I knew he was no more in that room than the poor couple's dead daughter. I forced myself to remember not my own loss but the task at hand.

'Ah,' she said. In my mind, I recited all that Penelope had told me of herself. It was quite a list. She was very much more exciting than I.

Lilias suddenly threw her head back. Her eyes rolled until only the whites could be seen. The servant rushed forward and tied her arms to the chair and she threw herself about, her hair sticking to the sweat on her face and neck.

Something white issued from her mouth. Like smoke and like substance, in the half-light, it emerged and swirled. Then she spoke, her voice high-pitched as a girl. 'Oh, a woman weaves her webs and men dry up in the silk strands. How many hearts lie crushed under her feet? Should their names be told?'

I imagine if I had been Penelope, I would have said yes. Her life, as I say, is more exciting than mine. She was happy to admit it. But I said nothing. It was not hard to quiver as a guilty woman might, and despite all my common sense, I was on some primitive level terrified. Penelope's maid cleared her throat, and Lilias's eyes flickered and her lips pursed as if irritated. I think perhaps Penelope's maid and Ada are related.

With a sharp cry Lilias collapsed in her chair, fallen forward in the restraints. The lights came on and the servant ushered us out.

'She is exhausted,' he said. 'The spirits drain her. But no doubt they will contact you soon. Those of you who are open.' His eyes swept from the louche man to Penelope's maid.

***

The exchange between me and Penelope was easier and more dignified in the dark. It involved the normal sort of climbing in and out. Penelope had had a wonderful evening with Margaret, no doubt filling her head with potential exploits to make your aunt Alice's hair curl, and then she, dressed as me, had been collected to go out again. If anyone was following, they were lost in the West End. In the comfort of Sam's cab, I changed back into my own things and removed the false fringe. *The Empire.* The young man had secrets to sell and a need or desire for wealth. Whose secrets? Which empire? It felt as if we were on the right track. But still, in spite of the spring warmth, I was chilled to the bone.

And although I am not fanciful, perhaps in my heart I knew that something was wrong. For I was still shivering when I walked up the steps, and nearly fell through the front door as Ada wrenched it open with bound hands. She was gagged and she shook like a dog as I pulled it loose.

'Get the police!' she cried. 'Miss Margaret's been taken!'

CHAPTER 20
Connie

Albert's father was as good as his word. A letter had arrived for Albert in the lunch-time post on Saturday, and when he opened it I saw *Coutts* at the head of the page. He skimmed the letter, then passed it to me. 'Anstruther's doing more than he needs,' he remarked.

The letter was written in a neat, sloping hand which had had all its quirks rubbed away by years of ledger-work.

Dear Mr Lamont,

Your father came to see me this morning and requested the transfer of the monies which you have been managing for him back to his sole control. He was in a state of some agitation, and I advised him to sleep on the matter, but he would not be dissuaded.

I am afraid that I told a slight untruth and advised him that you would also be required to sign a release document, and that it was too late to summon you today, in the hope that he will rethink his decision. He was most displeased, but agreed to return first thing on Monday morning to complete the process.

I hope that a Monday meeting is convenient for you, and that this transfer can be forestalled.

Sincerely,

J Anstruther

'He's going to do it, isn't he?' I said, giving back the letter.

'He is.' Albert shrugged. He looked — not quite sad, more resigned. 'I think Moss is in a bit of a spin. Father wasn't shy of bragging about how well his investments were doing, and I've gone and pulled the rug from under his feet.'

'Whose feet?'

'Both of them.' He rubbed at the frown between his eyebrows, but it remained. 'Father's little secret is out, and Moss's expectations of a sizeable inheritance may be modified now that he knows what a loose cannon Father is.' He sighed. 'Connie, I have a favour to ask.'

'Of course, what is it?'

'Will you accompany me to the bank on Monday?'

I tried not to shiver as I imagined Mr Lamont's glowering face. 'I don't think your father will want me there.'

'Hang my father.' Albert reached for my hand. 'I'm hoping that if you come, he will at least behave. And so shall I. If he goads me — and I think he will —' The frown deepened.

'Of course I'll come.' I squeezed his hand. 'I can go on to the office afterwards.'

'Oh yes.' Albert's smile was like sunshine breaking through a stormy day. 'You're keeping the troops in order.'

***

I dressed carefully on Monday morning. A dress of good quality, but not extravagantly trimmed; a modest hat; sensible boots. Not only did I want to look like someone who might possibly be in charge of a government bureau, I also wished to avoid any conspicuous display of wealth in front of Albert's father.

Albert came in as I was pinning my hat. He was wearing his usual dark suit and silk tie, and I reflected on how much easier these matters were for men. 'You look very . . . *appropriate*, my dear,' he said, smiling.

'I'm glad you noticed,' I managed to say, before he kissed me and almost disarranged the hat completely. 'Albert!' I reproved, setting it straight.

An audible tut came from the bedroom, where Violet was rolling stockings.

'Come along, we'd better go.' Albert offered his hand. 'Father's mood won't improve for waiting.'

It was a short drive to the bank, and neither of us spoke. I wondered if Albert felt as apprehensive as I did. If so, he didn't show it; his expression was thoughtful, rather than worried. 'Here we are, sir,' called Tredwell. 'Shall I wait?'

'Please,' said Albert. 'I don't think we'll take long.'

The same flunkey as always stepped forward. Was it my imagination, or was his welcome a little less effusive than usual? 'Mr Lamont, wonderful to see you, and Mrs Lamont too.' Suddenly I wished I had worn my best dress and every item of jewellery I possessed, as armour. 'Do come this way.'

Our footsteps were noiseless on the thick carpet. 'You'll still come here and make the right decisions,' I murmured, as we walked together. 'You'll still meet Mr Anstruther, and he'll give you a balance, and everything will be all right.'

Albert gave a tiny snort, and stopped suddenly. 'Oh Connie, you are lovely,' he said, looking into my eyes. 'But I'm not worried for myself.'

We reached Mr Anstruther's office. He opened the door immediately on the flunkey's knock. Albert's father was already seated, waiting. 'About time,' he grumbled. His brow lowered as he caught sight of me. 'This isn't an at-home or a dinner party, you know.'

'Constance has business in town, too,' said Albert. 'Shall we get on?' He set a chair for me, then sat down himself.

'Here are the documents,' said Mr Anstruther, indicating three sheets of paper laid out ready on the desk. 'There is a copy for each of you, and one for our files. Please read them carefully and sign where I have placed a cross. I shall act as witness.'

'A pretty show this, to have to claim your own money back,' huffed Mr Lamont. 'Perhaps I shall change my bank.'

'Perhaps you shall,' said Mr Anstruther, very calmly.

Mr Lamont's eyes flicked over the paper, and he held out his hand for a pen. Mr Anstruther, eyebrows raised, put one into his hand, and he scrawled his signature; once, twice, thrice. 'There,' he said, looking round at his son. 'Your turn, Bertie.'

'My name is Albert, father.'

'Called you Bertie when you were a lad, and as far as I'm concerned you still are.'

Albert looked at his father. 'Perhaps that's the problem,' he said quietly, before reading the documents. 'That seems to be in order,' he said, uncapping his fountain pen. 'Anstruther, just to clarify, I wish you to keep the two accounts entirely separate. I know you have a ledger for each, but there must be no risk of confusion between my personal holdings and my father's.'

'That is quite in order,' said Mr Anstruther. 'In fact, I anticipated that you would make the request, and therefore I have taken steps. Mr Lamont, your account will be transferred to a colleague of mine, a very capable man called Baines. I know that he will take care of you.' But he wasn't looking at Albert. He was looking at Albert's father.

'What? What?' Mr Lamont burst out. 'Why isn't *he* being moved?'

'In that case,' said Albert, with a gleam in his eye, 'I am entirely satisfied.' Pen touched paper, and the deed was done.

***

Maurice Lamont came to supper that evening, and Mrs Jones, warned that we had company, produced a nicely-cooked four courses. 'See,' I whispered to Albert, 'she *can* do it, when she concentrates.'

However, Johnson could have served the sole of a boot garnished with potato peelings for all the notice Maurice took of the food. 'It's just so sudden,' he said, waving a piece of turbot impaled on his fork. 'To find out my little brother is some sort of business magnate, and my father's a windbag. Well, I knew he was a windbag, but now he's proved it.' He darted a glance at me. 'Sorry to be rude about the old man, Connie, but really.'

'It's quite all right, Maurice,' I said, trying not to laugh. 'Parents can be . . . difficult.'

'Oh, do call me Moss,' said Maurice. 'Otherwise I feel far too much like Father.'

'So what do you want to do?' Albert asked.

Moss lounged in his chair. 'As you know, Albert, I'm hardly flush. However, I do have a little spare cash in the three percents, and I'd like you to invest it for me.'

Albert put down his cutlery. 'Are you sure?'

Moss waved his still-uneaten fish at the dining room in general. 'Seems to have worked out for you.'

'Very well.' Albert smiled. 'We can talk it over after dinner if you like. We shall need to draw up an agreement —'

A loud knock at the front door, and I heard the maid bustle past. 'I wonder who that is,' I said thoughtfully. 'Perhaps Mina, back from her s —, um, appointment.'

A tap at our door, and Nancy entered. 'It's a telegram for you, ma'am,' she said, handing it to me. 'Shall I wait?'

'Please.' I ripped it open. Could it be that Jemima had finally given birth?

It was a different kind of news entirely. *Margaret snatched from home come at once Mina.*

I gasped. 'Oh my God!'

'What is it?' Albert got up and came to me. 'Is it Jemima? Or the baby?' He tried to put his arms round me but I shook my head.

'They've taken Margaret!' I stood up. 'We must go there at once.'

'Who?' said Moss. 'Our cousin Margaret?'

'Yes,' Albert replied. 'Johnson, tell Tredwell to get the carriage out. Moss, you'll have to come with us. I'd drop you at your rooms, but there isn't time.'

'Sir, yes sir,' quavered Johnson, fleeing the room.

A ball of fear was growing in the pit of my stomach. Why had they taken Margaret? What did the mediums and the mind-readers have to gain from that? What would they do to her? And it had happened while I was in charge. I had promised Katherine that I would look after everyone, and I had failed. I buried my face in my hands, but a little voice said to me: *You're in charge.* I couldn't cry. I had to step up, and find her. 'I'll get changed,' I said. 'If we're running round the streets of London, I'm doing it in comfortable shoes.'

'Good point, Connie,' said Albert. 'Put something warm on.'

Suddenly a volley of bangs sounded on the front door, as if someone was trying to batter it down. I hurried to see — then stopped. What if they were coming for me, too? But a voice screamed 'Let me in!'

A girl's voice.

Margaret's voice.

I wrenched the door open and Margaret tumbled in. Her hair was loose, her face streaked with dirt, and her eyes were wild. I helped her into the dining room, put her in a chair, and sent Johnson for brandy. 'What happened, Margaret?' I asked, softly. She was still panting for breath. 'Are you all right?'

Margaret nodded, and as her breath slowed she took in the table, the meal, and Moss. 'Sorry to come at a bad time,' she gasped. She had recovered enough to manage a cheeky grin.

I grinned back. 'You could just ask for an invitation, you know.'

Johnson returned with a glass of brandy and Margaret managed to drink a little, though her teeth chattered on the rim of the glass. 'Penelope had gone,' she said, setting the glass on the table. 'A minute or two later, there was a knock. I thought she must have forgotten something. Opened the door, and someone put a sack over my head. I shouted, and Ada came running, but she screamed "Men in hoods!" as I was dragged down the steps. I tried to fight but there were two of them, and they pulled me up some carriage steps and dropped me on the floor. Then one of them said he had a knife and he'd use it if I screamed. So I didn't. The door banged shut and someone else came into the carriage. Then we drove off.'

'Good heavens,' said Moss.

'I asked them what they were going to do with me, and one of them said "We're taking you to a meeting with the person you seek." I said that I wasn't seeking anyone, and then they seemed to be conferring. One of them pulled the sack off my head, said something very impolite, and put it back on. "Right," he said. "If you don't want a meeting, we'll drop you off here." He shouted to the driver, and I felt the sack tighten round my neck. I would have screamed but I was busy trying to kick him. "Just tying your bonnet strings, miss," he said, and I swear he was laughing. The wheels sounded as if we were on gravel; then I heard the door open, and they threw me out. When I got the sack off I was in the middle of a deserted park. I got to the road, remembered you lived near, and ran as fast as I could.' She picked up the glass and drained it.

I got up and rang the bell. 'Johnson, go and tell Violet to run a hot bath. Miss Demeray will stay with us tonight. When you've done that, wire Mina Robson and tell her that we have Margaret safe, and that Tredwell will collect her and Ada as soon as he can.' Johnson fled, looking a little confused. 'Margaret, would you like something to eat?'

Margaret nodded; she might have been as confused as Johnson but nothing ever slowed her appetite. 'Good,' I said, ringing the bell. 'I'll ask Mrs Jones to work a miracle and divide three into four.'

Moss cleared his throat. 'Excuse me, Connie, but — what just happened?'

I sighed. 'Oh, this is normal, Moss. Kidnappings, escapes, and unexpected guests. But at least the food's quite nice.' I met Albert's eyes, and he grinned.

Chapter 21
Katherine

Far below, waves crashed and swirled. Beyond and beyond the grey sea, flecked with white, rolled in towards the mouth of the estuary. From the cliff top I looked down on the castle and the little church. The skies above threatened, and there was a whisper of rain in the wind which tangled my hair. But I didn't care. James's arms came round my waist and pulled me close. His fingers slipped between the buttons on my jacket and caressed me through my thin blouse.

'Oh dear, where 'as your corset gone?' he murmured, nuzzling my ear and kissing my neck. 'Did you leave it in Dorset specially?'

I couldn't believe the wonder. Every one of my senses overwhelmed me. I could smell the salty waves, taste the sun hidden behind the cloud, hear James's pulse quicken to keep time with mine, and when I turned in his arms I was intoxicated by his love, his wonderful love. I was lost in him and yet the world, even under rainy skies, was glorious.

'I love you,' he said, his hand caught in my plait. 'You will never know how much. I loved you from the moment you first kissed me. Oh, Katherine...' We kissed, alone on the cliff top, as if there were no other people, no London, no Dartmouth, no little cottage on the hillside, high above the harbour.

'Let's go back,' I whispered. It would be warm inside, and we would be alone. James had organised a maid to make and clear an evening meal. For the rest of the time we lived on bread, jam, tea, cheese, wine and each other. It would be warm by the hearth, wrapped in each other's arms.

***

The next day, at breakfast, I was not hungry.

'What's wrong?' James caught my hand and ran his thumb across it.

'I wish we didn't have to start home on Thursday.'

'I wish we didn't have to go home at all.'

'Don't you?'

For a moment I imagined us living here for ever. No more dirty streets and choking, foggy air. No more work. No more family to look after, or friends to encourage to do what they *could* do, if only they believed in themselves... I sighed.

'When we're back it will be fine,' said James, as if convincing himself. 'Come and sit on my lap while there's still just the two of us.'

'I'm sorry. Margaret is my responsibility. I can't

abandon her.'

'And it's her home. I know. I don't mind. At least we won't be like Connie and Albert, never knowing when a maid will walk into the room.' He paused. 'Ada won't bring us morning tea, will she?'

'Ada? Only if we're at death's door.' I snuggled into his neck. 'I'm tired,' I said.

'Me too, you're wearing me out every night.'

I giggled and then sighed. 'I didn't sleep well.'

'Something's bothering you, isn't it?'

I nodded. 'I'm not sure what. If anything was wrong someone would write, wouldn't they?'

'No one knows where we are,' said James.

'Oh.'

'Tell you what, let's go into Dartmouth. Get a change of scene, buy some presents, have a lunch that's not cheese-based. Come on, get dressed you hussy.'

***

We arrived at the quay at noon. James lifted me down from the trap, dislodging my hat. Or perhaps it was askew anyway. I hadn't worn one for two days.

'I didn't expect you to get this dressed up,' grumbled James. 'You're all starched and inaccessible again.'

'I can't wander round town half-naked,' I argued.

'Being corsetless under a jacket and having your hair down hardly constitutes nakedness.'

A passing woman glared. 'Shh,' I said.

We walked arm in arm along the quay, warm in the spring sun, listening to the ferrymen call out for passengers, watching the train puff into Kingswear. On

Saturday afternoon we had arrived at the same station, and in two days we would be heading home.

'Do you think we can empty the carriage on the way back like we did on the way here?' said James. 'Your kissing has improved no end. But I think you still need practice.' He dipped his head and pressed his lips to mine. 'In fact,' he murmured, 'if we really wanted to be left alone, we could always…'

I burst out laughing and another old lady glared. Would there ever be a time when no-one cared if people embraced in public? It seemed unlikely. We gave up, reverted to proper behaviour and went for lunch at the hotel. My sense of unease still fluttered, but I distracted myself watching passers-by through the window, wondering who were locals and who were visitors.

'Shall we buy a paper?' said James.

I shook my head. 'Let's keep the world out a little longer.'

James gestured round the room. 'Do you wish we'd stayed here in luxury?'

'No. I love our little cottage. You're all I want.'

'Let's go back,' said James. 'The sun's shining. Let's go back, get a blanket and go out to the cliff again. Let's scare the rabbits and stay out until the sun sets.'

***

The following morning we didn't get up till nearly ten. James unwrapped the bread the maid had left the night before, and gasped.

'What is it?' I asked.

His face had paled. For a moment I thought he was

going to pretend that all was well, but we had promised honesty. He pulled his chair round and held out the wrapping, it was an inner sheet from the previous day's London paper.

UNKNOWN ASSAILANTS ATTACK LADY

A young lady is recovering with friends after she was attacked in her own home in Mulberry Avenue, Fulham. The eighteen year old was abducted, but shortly afterwards released in a park, and managed to find her way to friends in Marylebone. She was unhurt in the attack, the reasons for which remain a mystery. Her maid was also attacked, but is likewise unhurt.

The assailants are described as two men of average height and build. No more could be seen as they were disguised with hoods. Their class and origin is uncertain. Young ladies are reminded that they should at all times ensure they have a male guardian to protect them...

'Margaret?' I said. *My little sister.* 'Ada?'

'Get dressed,' said James. 'We'll send a wire to Albert and wait at the telegraph office until we get a reply. Try not to worry. If it is Margaret she's safe, and I pity the man who tries to best Ada.'

***

Hours later, filthy and aching from the train, I flung my arms round Margaret in Connie's dainty morning room. We stood for a while, hugging, the smuts from my face smearing on hers.

'Oh Kitty, you shouldn't have come back,' she said. 'I'm quite well. You shouldn't have spoiled your honeymoon.'

'I can't leave you for five minutes,' I said, stroking her auburn hair away from her face. 'All you had to do was look after Ada.'

'She is so angry. She's reading your book on self-defence and she wants James to teach us ju-jitsu. No one is going to do that to us again and get away with it.'

'Are you really all right? Is Ada?'

'Stop fussing,' said Margaret, giving me one last hug. 'You're making me grubby.'

'When are you coming home? Can you get your things?'

'Not till tomorrow,' said Connie. 'Nor you. Violet has run you a bath and is laying clean things out in the jade room. I won't hear of you and James travelling any more today. Cook will have supper waiting. Ada came today to give Margaret a piece of her mind for gallivanting with strange men with a bag over her head, and she gave Cook a piece of her mind too when she saw what was being prepared for lunch. She's gone home, but Mina will be here shortly.'

***

I felt more human after a soak in the bath. I chuckled, thinking of the tin tub in front of the fire in the cottage, imagining Violet's face if she came in with more towels and found James scrubbing my back, soaping my shoulders. Or worse.

James had bathed in one of the other bathrooms. I

helped him with his collar studs and he helped me pin up my hair. For a moment we sighed. The cliff top seemed a lifetime ago and a million miles away. We kissed and, arm in arm, went downstairs to the dining room.

'Have you told the police what you suspect?' I asked in the drawing room later. Albert had asked James to stay behind for brandy and cigars. It was unlike either of them, but Albert looked troubled. In the drawing room the wine was good, and I held Margaret's hand as if she was still a child. She didn't let go.

'No,' said Mina. 'It's still too tangled yet, but it's becoming clearer. Anyway, you shouldn't be worrying about it. Connie has everything in hand and you are still on honeymoon.'

I glanced over at Connie. She had that look which meant she was desperate to say a million things and anxious with the effort to say nothing.

'No, I'm back now. We need to get to the bottom of this. James and I can finish our honeymoon another time.'

Connie exhaled. 'Well…' she said.

'I thought they were following us,' said Mina. 'Someone was here during the reception. They must have known who was getting married, so why did they kidnap Margaret? Then I realised they thought she was me. We are about the same height and build. You forget Margaret is eighteen now. In the hallway, which is dark, we'd have looked very similar.'

'But where were you at that time of night?'

Mina explained about her visit to Lilias. Even in the bright cosiness of Connie's drawing room, I felt chilled.

'But someone was following you too. This seems excessive for tax evasion and fraud.'

'It's more than that,' said Connie. 'There's blackmail, we think, and —'

'Secrets being stolen and sold,' said Mina. 'There is a link between the Department and two of our people. Vitruvius and Lilias.'

'Vitruvius…' I said.

'Keep thinking,' said Connie. 'It took us all day, but we worked it out.'

'A letter came for you,' said Margaret suddenly. 'We didn't know if it was relevant. I wanted to open it but the others said no.' She handed me a letter in a mauve envelope. It was addressed to Mrs King. *Private*.

I opened it, expecting to read something from a medium or mesmerist, but I was wrong. It was from Geraldine Timpson.

Dear Mrs King, it said, *I write to apologise for my unforgivable behaviour. I still fear for your children, but perhaps I was mistaken about your sister-in-law's condition, and should not have listened to gossip. I wish you well with a husband who will doubtless cherish you. I beg you not to tell Mr Timpson what you know of my connection with The Sphinx.*

Yours sincerely,
Mrs Timpson

I frowned, then read the last sentence aloud. 'Why should she be worried if her husband knows she was at the matinee?'

Connie and Mina exchanged glances.

'If that was all she did,' said Connie.

'Ernestine had a word with some of the stage assistants,' said Connie. 'Mrs Timpson left the theatre with Vitruvius.'

'How curious,' I said. 'Do we assume Mr Timpson is cruel, or a cuckold?'

'Or is he of interest to Vitruvius, perhaps?' asked Connie.

'I have no idea,' I said. 'But I'm sure we can find out.'

'Have you worked out Vitruvius yet?' asked Connie. 'What was the other name you found familiar? Come on, your mind can't be that befuddled with love.'

I looked askance at her, then closed my eyes. The penny dropped. 'Vaughan Treeves. Andrew's stepdaughter's husband.'

Connie clapped.

'Yes. A whole day in Somerset House and newspaper archives. He is indeed. He was a gentleman with a private income. Several suits for breach of promise, accusations of seduction, families paid off. The money dribbled away. After he married Miss Gwinnett, he turned his parlour tricks into his profession. And then, of course, young Max got work in the Department.'

'Have you found Max yet?'

'In a manner of speaking, yes,' said Mina, sipping

her wine. 'He's still on the payroll, with a desk in three sections. Each one thinks he's in the other. It's been like that for nine years. Everyone thinks he's somewhere else. No one knows where he actually is.'

Chapter 22
Connie

'How does it feel?' Albert whispered in my ear.

'How does what feel?' I replied, turning over and snuggling closer to him. It felt very strange to have to whisper in one's own home, but I felt surrounded by people; Katherine, James, Margaret, and Mina, all under the same roof as us. They might be asleep, they might not. I had a distinct feeling that Katherine and James were not.

'Handing back the reins.' Albert stroked my hair.

'To Katherine, you mean?'

'Mm.'

'I'm not sure. I thought I'd be relieved, but...'

'Ah well, now you've had a taste of power —' I could hear his smile; but there was a trace of something else there, too.

'Did you and Moss come to an arrangement?' I asked. It was the first chance I had had to speak to him alone since we had got up that morning. We had either been surrounded by our guests, or working.

Albert settled himself more comfortably. 'We did,' he said. 'We'll start him in low-risk stocks with a few speculations, and review monthly.' He laughed, quietly. 'I think he forgets that I've been managing the family money for a few years, but of course this is new to him.'

'Have you heard anything more from your father?'

A rustle. 'Nothing.' His voice was neutral.

'I'm sorry, Albert.'

'Don't be. It isn't your fault, or anyone's but his own.' His sigh tickled my forehead. 'Moss asked if he could tell the others. I said yes.'

'Perhaps you'll end up with a new portfolio of investments to manage.' I spoke lightly; but in my head I saw a queue of Lamonts outside Albert's study door.

'Not if it interferes with us,' Albert said, and while he spoke in an undertone, I heard the determination in his voice. 'Speaking of interfering...' His hand stopped stroking my hair, and moved between my shoulder-blades, down my spine —

I gasped. 'With all these people in the house?' I squeaked.

'Don't you want to?'

'That isn't the point. I mean — ooh! — I mean — oh never mind.'

***

Our guests departed after breakfast. Mina was first to go. 'I shall see you at the office,' she said as she got up from the table. 'I think these two would like a little space.' Katherine looked up, half-indignantly, then subsided into gazing at James while he buttered his toast. I wondered if I had ever been so obviously lovestruck, and decided that yes, I probably had.

'You'll manage if I don't come in today, won't you?' asked Katherine, blushing. 'I'd hoped for a week's leave, and James has to move his things in. And I'd like to be home when Margaret gets back from school.'

'That's perfectly all right,' I replied. 'Mina and I are managing very well.'

'Good,' said James. 'I need Katherine to do the heavy lifting.'

'Don't worry,' said Margaret. 'Ada and I shall make sure there aren't any, um, accidents.' She began to giggle and Katherine shot her a look which said, as plainly as words, *I'll deal with you later.*

I heard Mina coming downstairs and went into the hall to say goodbye. 'Thank you very much for having me, Connie,' she said, as if she had been at a party. 'I shall drop my things off at home, then proceed to the office.' She held out her gloved hand, and when I took it a folded square of paper pressed against my palm. Mina nodded to me, and Johnson, bowing in rather a cowed way, opened the door for her.

I waited until Johnson had gone back into the morning room before reading the note. *Today at the office I propose a game of hide-and-seek*, Mina had written. *Dress down. As close to what the typing girls wear as possible, please.*

I caught sight of myself in the hall mirror — my this-season day dress, my jewellery — and crumpled the note in my palm. I would have to wait till the others had gone to comply.

***

Mina was already at the office when I arrived, dressed in a drab grey calico and a black jacket with distinct wear at the elbows. She looked me over. 'You'll do,' she said crisply. 'For you, I suppose that *is* dressed down. Barely a diamond or an ostrich feather in sight.'

'Tell me about this game of hide-and-seek.' I perched on the edge of my desk, too excited to even type a word.

'Well,' said Mina. 'It occurred to me that, while we have lots of pieces of the jigsaw, and they are beginning to fit together in a very plausible pattern, there is one large piece missing.'

'Which is?'

'Andrew.' Mina sighed. 'Or, more precisely, his lost work. He was, first and foremost, a methodical man. Precise, orderly, neat. All those things that sound so dull to young people like yourself and Katherine.'

'But didn't Mr Maynard say that Andrew lost things? Reports?' The words were out of my mouth before I could stop myself, and I could see the pain in Mina's face. I had as good as contradicted her, the woman who knew him better than anyone.

'Yes, he did say that,' Mina replied, quietly. 'But there is a difference between something being truly lost, and being put where no-one can find it.'

'So you think he hid the reports? But why?' I felt bad all over again. While I respected Mina's calm intelligence, could her perception have been blurred by her love for Andrew Fowler?

'You think I am grasping at straws.' Humour flashed in Mina's grey eyes.

'No, no, I —'

'Connie.' She smiled. 'I wasn't born yesterday. You are easy to read as a book.'

'But if he did hide the reports, and no-one has ever discovered them — not as far as we know — how will we find them?'

'Our fourth team member has been sadly underused,' remarked Mina.

'Ernestine?' I frowned. 'How will she be able to tell where Andrew Fowler hid his papers?'

'It is a long shot, I admit,' said Mina. 'But I have a feeling that, somehow, I know.'

***

'You aren't going to hypnotise her or anything, are you?'

Ernestine Bugg had placed two chairs on either side of one of the tables, and cleared the typewriter out of the way. Mina sat very composedly, her hands turned palm-up on the table.

Ernestine shot me a scornful look. 'Mrs L, you know I ain't one of them smoke-and-mirrors people.' Gently, she took hold of Mina's hands. 'Could you close your eyes for me, Mina?'

Mina did as she was told, and I took a step back.

'So, Mina, you reckon Mr Fowler hid some reports, or information.'

'I do.' Mina inclined her head.

'Tell me why you think that.'

'Andrew was tidy. He never lost things. Ever. Even when he was —' She swallowed. 'Even when he was troubled, he was neat in person.'

'A place for everything,' said Ernestine.

'Yes. That's why, thinking about it now, I don't believe that he mislaid that information. I think he put it where it couldn't be found before he was ready.'

'But why?' I asked.

Ernestine shushed me with a glare. 'But why, Mina?' she repeated.

'Perhaps it wasn't ready,' Mina said, dreamily. 'Perhaps he didn't have everything he needed.'

'What else did he need?'

'Proof. He needed proof. And he was close to getting it. That is why he died.' She opened her eyes, and they were wet with unshed tears.

'Let's go back to the information,' said Ernestine softly, and Mina's eyes closed again. 'You think it was on paper, not in his head.'

'Yes. He was always a man to write things down. Appointments, birthdays, memoranda.'

'Which department did he work in, Mina?'

'Foreign Reciprocals.'

'Would he have taken the information out of the building?' Ernestine's green eyes were fixed on Mina, unblinking. It was as if she was trying to see into Mina's mind.

Slowly, Mina shook her head. 'No. He would not.'

'Could he have hidden it in another department?'

'He could, but he wouldn't. Too risky.'

'So where is it, Mina?' Ernestine's voice dropped to a whisper.

'It is in the office.' Mina's voice rang out clear. 'It is in the Foreign Reciprocals office. Hiding in plain sight. Like Andrew and I used to be. It is all of a piece.' Mina's eyes snapped open. She snatched her hands away from Ernestine's and put them to her head. 'Why did I never see this before?'

'No one ever asked you before,' said Ernestine matter-of-factly. 'Would you like a cup of tea?'

'No. No.' Mina took Ernestine's hands again. 'I want to go on.'

'Do you know what the Foreign Reciprocals office looks like, Mina?'

Mina closed her eyes in thought, and her breathing grew slower, more shallow. 'I have seen it. Not often. I met Andrew once or twice in the office, after hours, in summer. I did not dare to visit when other people were there. It is a large room, full of desks and chairs and card indexes and cabinets. And dust. They try to keep it clean, but inevitably dust collects with the papers, and the files. The motes rise and play and catch the sun which shines through the high windows. They dance in its slanting beams.'

'What else can you tell me about the room, Mina?'

'It is like an oven in the heat of full sun. Andrew told me that sometimes, even in the day, they have to draw the curtains because of the unbearable heat, and loosen their neckties.'

'What are the curtains like?'

'Thick, and dark. They blot out the light completely.' I imagined Andrew Fowler closing the curtains to hide himself and Mina. 'They smell as if they are made of dust and tobacco smoke.'

'Is there a carpet in the office, Mina?'

Mina shook her head. 'Parquet. Carpet would wear too much.'

'Where do you think the information is hidden, Mina?'

Mina met Ernestine's eyes with hers, and they were clear and untroubled. 'Somehow, Andrew has hidden it in the curtains. He would not trust it to a file. All the cabinets have a duplicate key. All the desks are to the same pattern. There is nowhere else it could be.' She sighed a long, long sigh. 'That feels better.'

'But how shall we get it out?' I asked. 'We can hardly barge into the Foreign Reciprocals office and start cutting up their curtains.'

'No,' said Mina, though she didn't sound too averse to the idea.

'Where is the office?' asked Ernestine, in her normal, sharp voice.

'It is on the first floor, and it has just one door. We would definitely be spotted.'

'Unless we, too, went after hours.' I said. A germ of an idea was growing in my brain.

'But how?'

'There are a whole group of people whom I have

never seen, but I know they work here.' Mina and Ernestine both raised their eyebrows at me. 'Someone must clean the offices.'

'Yes, they must,' said Mina. 'Although I'm not sure we'd notice if they didn't.'

'Or could we ask Mr Maynard to get us in there?' I wondered aloud.

Mina frowned. 'I'm not sure his remit extends to burgling other departments, Connie.'

'That's a pity. But we could ask him when the housekeeping staff come.'

There was a definite twinkle in Mina's eye. 'Yes. That would be an entirely different matter.'

***

'Go on,' said the charlady, 'leave yer little note. I ain't one to stand in the way of true love.' She spun the shilling I had given her in her lean hand while I hurried into the Foreign Reciprocals office, clutching a white envelope addressed to Mr Fitzherbert in the most ornate script I could manage.

The door clicked behind me, and my footsteps echoed in the cavernous space. *Three minutes*, I thought. *I only have time to walk to a desk, place a letter on it, and go.* Or the charlady would hear my footsteps this way and that, and grow suspicious, and —

Stop it, Connie.

I stopped, and looked at my feet. Then I stepped out of my shoes, and padded towards the high windows. Standing on tiptoe, I ran my hands down the length of the drawn curtains, one hand on the dark, slubbed cotton, one on the thinner lining.

Nothing in the first.

Nothing in the second.

Nothing in the third.

And so on, and so on, till I came to the darkest corner of the office, and my palm felt a slight rise, a slight bulge, underneath the lining. Out came my sewing kit, and I nipped the stitches away. A few moments more, and I slipped a large, blank envelope into my bag. I ran to my abandoned shoes, and hurried to the door, where I found the charlady leaning on her mop, having mopped a circle round herself.

'Thank you so much,' I gasped. 'I couldn't find the right desk at first. I've left the note in his drawer. Oh, I *do* hope he notices me!' And I fled down the stairs, followed by the charlady's laughter.

Mina was waiting in a coffee house round the corner. She raised her eyebrows, and I nodded. 'Let's get a cab.'

We waited until we were safe at home before opening the envelope. 'What if it isn't anything to do with us at all?' I asked. 'What if —'

Mina took the envelope from me and ripped it open, drawing out several sheets of closely-written paper. 'This is Andrew's writing,' she said.

I hope that this never needs to be read, that this never needs to be used. If it is, then something has happened to confirm my fears...

And our eyes skimmed the pages, taking in Andrew Fowler's terrible tale.

CHAPTER 23
Katherine

We deposited Margaret at school, much to her disgust, although she cheered up when James asked if she'd told her friends of the kidnap and escape. I suspected that by noon everyone would believe she had wrestled the abductors to the ground with her bare hands and stolen their cab to drive to Connie's.

Then we went home. James helped me down from the carriage and waited.

'What's the matter?' I said. He was eyeing the neighbours' houses.

'Four curtains twitching,' he said, 'that'll do. Up you come!'

He swept me up in his arms and climbed the steps. As soon as Ada opened the door, he carried me over the threshold and dropped me on the mat.

'Oh my poor back,' he said. 'I never knew you were so heavy.' I kicked his shins.

Ada was grinning. She crushed us both in a wiry hug, did a little dance with us trapped in her arms, then let go. Her normal frown appeared and she put her hands on her hips. 'Finished gallivanting?'

'Finished wrestling with strange men?' asked James.

'Hmph. If I hadn't been looking for something in the pantry they'd never have got the better of me. Kidnappers indeed. They couldn't even do that properly, though trying to keep Miss Margaret under control has always been like holding a sack of squirrels.'

I hugged her again. 'I'm so glad you're safe, Ada.'

Her face dropped. 'I . . . I'm sorry I didn't keep her safe, Miss Kitty, I mean Mrs Katherine, I mean Madam.'

'Miss Kitty's fine, and no-one is blaming you. As you say, she can look after herself. I'm sorry you had to suffer. I fear I brought it on you.'

'Look on the bright side, Ada,' said James, taking our luggage from Tredwell. 'I bet nothing as exciting has ever happened to next door's Elsie.'

Ada waggled her head. 'That's true, Mr James, that's true.'

'And talking of the neighbours,' he continued, 'do they know Katherine is married now?'

'Possibly not. We don't talk to some of them.'

'Good. Nice to cause a scandal.'

Ada turned a deep crimson. 'I think we already have. The . . . er . . . new furniture arrived yesterday.'

For a second I wondered what she meant. James lived, or rather had been living, in a furnished flat. He was bringing only books and clothes. I couldn't imagine how he felt moving from bachelor neatness to the feminine clutter of our house. Then I remembered.

'Ah!' said James. 'Good. The new bed.' He nudged me and winked. I wouldn't have believed Ada could go any redder, but she did.

'I expect you'd like some tea,' said Ada, and clattered down the hall.

'Thank goodness,' said James. 'It was like standing between two tomatoes.'

I glanced at myself in the mirror and realised I looked worse than Ada.

'How are we going to…?'

'With caution,' said James. 'Come along, we'll sit in the drawing room and wait for our tea. Let's be a respectable married couple for an hour or so . . . then send Ada out on an errand.'

***

It was hard to believe I'd only been married for a week. I couldn't imagine not waking to find James curled up beside me, watching him breathe, knowing he was all mine. But it still felt odd to have him living in our house, sleeping with me in what had been Aunt Alice's room. In the end we'd gone out to dine, and spent the last night of our honeymoon in Brown's Hotel rather than sit with nonchalant Mina and smirking Margaret.

Today was a new day. James, although he didn't have to, went into the offices of the *Chronicle* while I returned home.

'Miss Robson left a message,' said Ada before I could take off my hat. 'She says please to meet her and Mrs Bertie at the park. She said you'd know which one.'

I groaned. 'Back in the harness, Ada.'

'I imagine so, Miss Kitty.'

I felt ashamed. It occurred to me that Ada hadn't been properly out of the harness for years. Once we'd solved the case I was going to give her a holiday, if I had to drag her to the seaside and tie her to a deckchair. It was time Margaret learned how to keep house.

***

The sun had come out. The air was still but soft, with floral scents from the park's borders. Mina and Connie were sitting on a bench waiting for me. Connie looked as if she might explode with news, but Mina was so still and her face so expressionless I knew she was in deep pain. I felt the sun's warmth seep away as she handed me a large, thick envelope and patted the bench.

I looked around. 'Are we still being followed?'

'I don't think so,' said Connie. 'I think they believe that either we took the hint when Margaret was abducted, or we're just incompetent. But…'

'But?'

'We need to move quickly. We must stop them before more lives get ruined.'

'The people they're blackmailing? The people like Andrew?'

'Not just them,' said Mina. 'The people who will be killed if they're not stopped. Little conflicts are being stirred up into big ones, to make rich men even richer.

Come on, Katherine, read the report.'

I hope that this never needs to be read, that this never needs to be used. If it is, then something has happened to confirm my fears.

This is the report of Andrew Fowler.

I joined the Department in 1862 at the age of nineteen. I was promoted several times and transferred to the Foreign Reciprocals section in 1875, shortly after marrying my widowed second cousin, Frances Gwinnett. I had neither means to marry before that date nor anyone with whom I wished to share my life, but my mother was insistent it was time to settle down. Franny was pleasant enough company although her children were troublesome. Her daughter Angelina was barely seventeen when she was seduced by Vaughan Treeves. I had been able to ensure he made an honest woman of her, but had not realised quite how impecunious he was, since he gave every impression of being, from the point of social standing at least, a gentleman. Franny's son Maximilian had been expelled from school and sent down from Oxford, but Franny convinced me that even though I was just twelve years older, I had a responsibility to find him suitable employment and a fresh start.

Against my better judgment, in 1877 I found him a job as a junior clerk in the Department, despite knowing he was unsuited to a repetitive, mundane, subservient role. Unsurprisingly he lived up, or should I say down to my expectations in a very short time. For several months only my interventions stopped his dismissal. Meanwhile Angelina's husband had made a name for himself as a mind-reader, entertaining the higher class of audience. I suspected chicanery, but their household needed some sort of income. I tried to keep a distance, but they were forever visiting us and asking me about work, though they knew I was bound to discretion. Sadly Max seemed all too keen to break those bounds. I was glad he was still at a junior level and had little understanding of the files passing through his hands. I absented myself from the conversations as much as possible.

When Franny died the following year, I shared her estate between Max and Angelina and told them both that I considered any responsibility towards them to be over and that they must forge their own paths from here on in.

In 1881 I met, for the first time, a woman who made my life complete. As soon as I am assured that my suspicions about the Department are wrong, <u>or</u> they have been put right, I shall marry her. I have left her separate information in a safety-deposit box in my bank. She will know the code, since it is the date we met. If I fear I am at great risk I shall tell her this in a letter, but I will not name her for fear that if this report is discovered, it may endanger her.

I looked up at Mina and swallowed, thinking of the love James and I had being snatched away. Tears came to my eyes, but her chin went up and she gave a tiny smile.

'Keep reading,' she said. 'He was a good man.'

'Yes,' I said, trying to keep my voice normal. 'Have you been to the bank?'

She nodded, and pointed at the report again.

It continued at length, setting out in neat clerk's handwriting dates, tables, notes of files mislaid for shorter or longer periods or missing altogether, sketch maps, names. The files related to reports of conflicts in obscure parts of the world which were being monitored by the Foreign Reciprocals section. Every one had great mineral or agricultural potential. The Department's interest seemed to be chiefly to protect trade interests and officials based on foreign soil.

Some of the conflicts appeared to be little more than local spats: family feuds, some going back centuries, which threatened to escalate. Others were more serious: tensions coming to a head because of economic pressures and political change. In every case, there were two potential paths: one in which diplomacy might settle things down, and another in which selling arms to one side would lead to a victory which would secure the entire mineral or agricultural profit for the winners.

There is a clear link between the loss of secret information, sales of arms by men who own armament companies, and trade agreements between companies owned by the same men and the recipients of the arms.

'But I don't see —'

'I found out what Mr Timpson does for a living,' said Connie, her voice very deliberately neutral.

I frowned. 'Geraldine's husband? What does it —'

'He trades in munitions.' Connie's face held an inward, quiet triumph.

'But then —'

'Keep reading.'

On the face of it, this seems coincidental. This is good business I daresay, if morally questionable. But what if the link does not simply anticipate conflict, but precipitates it? This would indicate to me that information is being sold. In which case, how?

There followed another table. The same list of dates, and an apparent change in Max's circumstances. He was still a junior clerk yet his address improved, his clothes were now bespoke, his shoes made to measure. He frequented the best restaurants and theatres, and grand soirées where respectable matrons appraised him for their upper-class but impoverished daughters.

'We've suspected all along that Max was selling secrets. And you found out the Sphinx was linked in somehow.'

'Keep reading.'

A third table. This one with the names of six men, their grade, and their length of service in the Department. Only two were from Foreign Reciprocals. Dates linked them with the files which had gone missing and an almost proselytising interest in the occult. Every one had become an aficionado of the Sphinx's stage act, and thereafter visited Lilias. Then, for most, a change in mood. Agitation, anxiety, depression, mania. One had retired, one had died suddenly in the office, one had asked to be stationed abroad and one was reputed to have committed suicide. Two, very young men at the time of writing, were still employed in the Department.

Had they sold information, or were they being accused of it and were afraid to say anything because someone had another hold on them? I must establish the truth.

Three months ago I found an unsigned letter in my drawer. The letter accused me of being responsible for missing information. I replaced it in my drawer with the intention of showing it to my senior manager later, but before I could do so, it disappeared.

Then Max sought me out and asked if I would go with him and Angelina to Vaughan's latest show for the sake of his mother, as it would have been her birthday. I was astonished at the effect Vaughan, or should I say Vitruvius, had. Quite sensible men and women trembled as he 'exposed' their innermost thoughts. It seemed to me that he simply picked notions that could apply to anyone. It was, however, very unnerving. Especially when he went into a 'trance' and said 'someone has lost something precious. If it is discovered, there will be great dishonour'. I was very disturbed and vowed never to return.

The following day, I found another letter in my drawer. Inside were two five-pound notes and a typed letter saying 'The dishonour may remain a secret.' Again I put it back in my drawer, intending to show my senior manager — and then I thought that if I played along, perhaps I might learn what was happening. I kept the money and waited. Nothing happened. I tried to find out if I was the only one, but no-one would discuss it. Files were mislaid and rediscovered, but everything else remained the same until another letter appeared. It said 'Of course, if you help, the dishonour will not be revealed. The Empire needs you'. I am uncertain. I am nearly prepared to go to a senior manager and explain my doubts. I fear I shall be dismissed, and have not yet worked out what to say. If only I can find the proof I need. I wish to marry the woman I love, and be left in peace.

And now Max, in great distress, says he has been troubled in a dream about his mother and asks me to accompany him to visit the medium Lilias Cadwalader. I shall go, but solely because there seems to be a link to this whole business. I do not believe in ghosts.

I put the letter down and looked at Mina.

'But somehow,' she said, 'Lilias convinced him otherwise, and bit by bit she destroyed him.'

'He was a good man,' I said.

Mina pulled off her right glove. On her ring finger was a beautiful gold ring with amethyst stones. I had never seen it before.

'Yes,' she said. 'This was to be my engagement ring. I never knew about the deposit box until I read this. There's no point in wearing it on my wedding finger now, but I shall treasure it and his last letter forever.' She handed me a note in the same neat script.

To my dearest darling Mina. If you read this, it is because they have silenced me. I should have married you when I realised I loved you, rather than take advantage of you. I fear I have dishonoured you and shall not have that exposed. Please forgive me. I did not think of it as dishonour, simply as impatience. I love you more than you can know.

Andrew

'He did not take advantage of me,' she said quietly, 'he did not dishonour me. I wanted to be with him as much as he did with me. I knew he loved me. I knew I was not just anyone.'

I held her hand. 'I know.'

'For them to make him think so breaks my heart. And I know what we'll do. We shall play them at their own game. I don't know quite how we shall manage it, ladies, but we are going to raise a ghost.'

Connie frowned. 'I really don't think —'

'Yes,' said Mina. 'We shall bring Andrew back when they're least expecting it, and *they* will tell the truth.'

Chapter 24
Connie

'Are you sure you'll be all right tonight?' Albert asked.

'I'll be fine,' I said, rather shortly. 'Mina will be with me, and you'll be close by.' I turned to the dressing table, and regarded myself in the mirror. Selina had been subtler this time, and while the wig still itched, at least I didn't look quite as odd as I had when I first saw myself at the music hall.

'You do look green, though. Even underneath all that.'

'Thank you for the compliment. Does Moss know you've borrowed his moustache, by the way?'

'Very funny.' Albert touched it self-consciously. 'I just hope it stays put.'

'I'd better not kiss you, then.' I managed to smile, though I felt queasy.

'No.' He smiled back, carefully. 'You'd smudge.'

***

Mina had requested another appointment as Penelope Bailey, and asked if she could bring a friend who had recently lost her son. She had painted me as a respectable lady of good standing, married to a Department worker, and I am afraid that we borrowed the name of a member of the Foreign Reciprocals staff, via Mr Maynard. Lilias's reply was swift, and in the affirmative.

Mina and Penelope had already arranged to perform their carriage switch again, and Selina would attend as my maid. Albert would loiter outside at a safe distance, watching for trouble or disturbance. Chief Inspector Barnes had been briefed. There was little more we could do to safeguard ourselves. Yet my stomach still churned as Selina and I rattled along with Tredwell. Oh, my stupid nerves.

'You'll be fine, Miss F — Mrs Lamont,' said Selina in her easy way, laying her hand on mine. 'Just sit back and enjoy the show.'

We arrived at Lilias's house in Chelsea a little early, and I instructed Tredwell to pull up a few yards short, and wait. Though Selina's calm presence was beginning to settle my nerves, I did not want to enter the house without Mina.

Mina's — or rather Penelope's — carriage came at five minutes to eight. Mina disembarked, dressed in black silk and wearing her false fringe, followed by a stern-faced woman who I presumed must be Penelope's maid. 'Ah, here you are, Cornelia,' she said. 'Let us go in together.' I took her arm gratefully; and while it appeared steady to the naked eye, I could detect a tremor beneath the stiffness.

A servant welcomed us and led us through the house to the room where the seance was to be held. It was as Mina had described it — the damask-covered table, the dim light, the heavy furniture — but I still felt completely unprepared. What if I was as scared as I had been at my first meeting with Bassalissa? What if I lost control of myself? Then I caught sight of a young man sitting opposite who looked more agitated than even I felt, and that reassured me a little. Lilias would not know who I was; she thought I was a grieving parent, and she would try to draw me in that way.

Gradually more people trickled in; an elderly couple, a woman in black who wrung her hands constantly, and an expensively-dressed, dissipated-looking man who seemed completely at odds with the rest of the company. They took their seats, and waited. I tried to catch Selina's eye, at the back of the room, but she was gazing at nothing with a beatific expression on her face. I remembered Ernestine thinking of sausage and mash when Vitruvius was reading her mind, and almost laughed aloud.

The door opened once more and Lilias was with us, a nondescript woman whose notable features were her loose hair and bare arms. Yet she had a presence in her stillness; her air of being not-quite-there made her interesting. She walked quietly to the chair left empty on one side of the table. Two servants followed her, and stood ready a few steps behind Lilias's seat. I noticed that it had arm-rests.

'Welcome, one and all,' Lilias said, rather faintly. 'Let us begin.' The servants dimmed the lights still further. Mina reached for my hand and squeezed it.

'Oh…' Lilias put her hands to her head. 'The spirits have much to say tonight. What is this?' She touched a glass set rim-down on the table, on a board ringed with letters. 'Someone help me.'

Mina and the dissipated young man put their fingers to the glass, and it moved to the initials *P* and *B*. 'PB,' said Mina. 'A message for PB.' She frowned, as if she were listening to words spoken far away. Then she turned to Mina. 'William forgives you,' she said. 'He says…' Her voice deepened suddenly. 'Time heals all things. I bear you no grudge for the things you said. I see now that you were right.'

'That is such welcome news,' said Mina gravely. 'I have often wondered…'

'Wonder no more. Be at peace.' Lilias heaved a long, shuddering sigh, and put her fingers to her temples in a way that reminded me of Vitruvius. I became aware of the scent of lilies, and a faint snatch of a harp playing.

'Mama?' Lilias said, in a thin high voice. 'Mama?'

I gasped. 'Tommy? Tommy!'

'Mama…'

'Oh, Tommy…' I stretched my hands forward as if I expected to touch my missing son. 'Where are you?'

'I am at the gate of Heaven, Mama.'

'The gate?'

'I cannot pass… They say something keeps me from

entering . . . something which ought to be told.'

'Something . . . which ought to be told?' I repeated, as if dumbfounded.

'Papa knows . . . remind him that his little Tommy is waiting, so patiently...'

'Ohh!' I wailed, and buried my face carefully in my hands, thanking Heaven myself for the dim light and sniffling as convincingly as I could.

'A message...' breathed Lilias. 'A message for . . . F?'

The agitated man's head jerked up. 'What is it?' he muttered. 'I have done all that I can.'

'There is room for more,' a deep voice intoned. 'You have not yet done enough to rest my spirit.'

The man quivered like a leaf in the wind. 'I dare not do more.'

'And you are right.' But it was not the same voice. It was less deep, less resonant, and it seemed to come not from Lilias, but from the glass on the table. 'You are right to disregard this spirit.'

A sort of squawk came from Lilias. I heard quick footsteps, and the lights rose a little. 'Oh, you cannot see me,' the voice said, sounding amused. 'I am a spirit, you know. I have delivered one message; but I have another. I have a message for MG.'

The dissipated-looking man started, and removed his hands from his pockets. 'What the —'

'Good evening, Max.'

The man sprang up. 'Who is this? Who's doing it?'

'Do you mean to say that you don't recognise my

voice? The voice of your own stepfather?'

Max backed away from the table. 'I — I —'

'So you do know me. Don't go, Max, I haven't finished with you. And I have so much to say. Do you hear that?'

A great rustling came out of nowhere, as if a thousand people were turning over the pages of a book.

'Paper. Paper everywhere. Valuable paper, inscribed with secrets. You like secrets, don't you, Max?'

Max shook his head. 'I don't know what you mean.'

'Call me by my name, if you please.'

Max glanced behind him, then ran to the door and wrenched at the handle, muttering to himself.

'You can't escape, Max. You drew me into this, and now it is my turn to draw you in…'

The other guests were muttering, glancing about restlessly.

'Do not be alarmed.' The voice rose slightly, added a touch of steel. 'I have no business with the rest of you. My *unfinished* business is with two people in this room; Maximilian Gwinnett and Lilias Cadwalader. Maximilian has betrayed his position and his country by obtaining and selling government secrets. Innocent people have died and will die, through conflict stirred up with the aid of this despicable man.'

'Quiet, Fowler,' growled Max. 'You can't prove a thing.'

'I have names,' said the voice. 'I wrote everything down.' All the lights went out, and an unearthly shriek came from where Lilias was sitting. Mina's hand tightened around mine.

'Candles! Light candles!' Lilias cried. There was a sudden rush of air from the window, and something blew into the room, rustling, flapping —

'Paper, paper everywhere. So many papers to file.' The voice had taken on a sarcastic tone. 'Poor Max, so bored, so badly paid, so unamused. But his brother-in-law could help, the sham mind-reader, and together they cooked up a plan, and brought this medium into it.'

'What did you expect?' Max cried. 'As if I was going to shuffle papers all day for a pittance.'

'It was an honourable position,' the voice said, sternly. 'Until you and Treeves dishonoured it. And when I began to work out what was happening, the pair of you tricked me into believing that my dead wife, your dead mother, wanted me to shield you.'

At last someone lit a candle, and brought it to the table. Lilias laughed, an unpleasant, mocking noise. 'You're not real,' she said, and her ethereal manner was quite gone. 'You're a fake.'

'Am I?' The sound of flapping paper returned. 'Well, you ought to be able to spot a fake, Miss Cadwalader. After all, it takes one to know one.'

Lilias emitted a low, animal sound and thrashed about in her chair. 'Spirit, begone!' she cried. 'Bind me! A new spirit is coming to speak through me, a powerful spirit, and I cannot answer for the consequences.'

Two servants stepped forward, drawing ropes from their pockets, but as they reached Lilias the candle was snuffed out in a breeze.

Lilias shrieked, and moments later, a deeper cry came from above our heads. I half-rose from my chair; but Mina grasped my wrist, and held me. 'It's all right,' she murmured.

'They preyed on my fears, my guilt at exposing my stepson,' the voice continued. 'This woman pleaded with me in the person of my dead wife. And when I decided I must tell the authorities about Max, he poisoned me with opium. He bought it from the druggist's shop round the corner from his office.'

'No I didn't,' said Max, scornfully.

'He remembers you.'

'He can't,' said Max, 'because I got it from the —'

The lights came back on at full strength, making us screw our eyes shut. When I could see again, Lilias was tied to her chair in such a manner that she could not get free. Maximilian Gwinnett was in the hands of a police officer. Chief Inspector Barnes stood near the door. The 'servants' standing by Lilias were, in fact, Katherine and Reg. And by the window stood James.

'I think we've heard all we need to,' said Chief Inspector Barnes. He turned to James. 'The name of the man you were impersonating?'

James looked a little shamefaced. 'Andrew Fowler.'

'And he did it very well,' said Mina, standing up and walking towards James. 'Thank you,' she said quietly, shaking his hand. 'Justice can now be done.'

'Let us hope so.' Chief Inspector Barnes surveyed the room. 'We shall take names and addresses, and I warn you that any of you may be called to bear witness in court to what happened here today. If you wouldn't mind leaving one by one, that's the quickest way.'

We filed out, and as I entered the hall I saw Vitruvius, dressed in shirt and trousers, sitting handcuffed on a chair, and next to him was Geraldine Timpson, wrapped in a cloak. The policeman standing next to them chuckled at my surprise. 'Caught 'em upstairs in bed, in a sight less than they're wearing now. I understand they're, ah, connected to the goings-on below.'

Geraldine bit her lip and studied the floor, and I didn't have the heart to say anything. Her reckoning would come soon enough.

***

'How did you do it?' I asked James, as Tredwell drove us home.

James grinned. 'Mr Templeton gave me a crash course in ventriloquism. Apparently if I ever want to swap journalism for a stage career, he'd be prepared to give me as much as a pound a week.'

'Stardom awaits,' said Katherine, mock-seriously. James slung an arm round her, and whispered something that made her giggle.

'The main thing is that it worked,' said Mina. Her face seemed to change every time I looked at her; first relieved, then joyful, then sorrowing, then at peace. 'I am so grateful to you.' Her forefinger touched the amethyst ring.

'And everyone's safe,' said Albert, squeezing my hand. 'Oh yes, and I can get rid of this thing.' He pulled at the edge of the moustache and winced. 'Or perhaps I'll wait till we get home.'

We dropped everyone else off, and it was only when Johnson answered the door and gasped at the pair of us that I realised we looked rather different from usual. 'Good evening, Johnson,' I said with dignity, sweeping past him into the hall. 'Don't worry, it is us. We were at a — costume party.' I removed my hat and pulled the wig off.

'A telegram came, ma'am,' he said, staring. 'It's on the salver.'

'For me?' I went across, wig in hand, and picked it up.

'There can't possibly be any more news, can there?' said Albert.

I picked up the letter-opener.

At long last we have a son Arthur Joseph 9pm Jemima doing well Charles.

'It's Jemima,' I managed to say. 'She's had the baby, and she's fine.'

'Oh good,' said Albert, coming to see the telegram and putting an arm round my shoulders.

'I — um — I need to go upstairs and clean myself up.'

'Yes, you do.'

Everything seemed to swim in front of me. I blinked, and clutched at the banister. 'Steady there!' Albert laughed. 'Should I carry you?'

Why wouldn't he understand? 'Come *along!*' I said, and, walking carefully, got myself to my boudoir. I dismissed Violet, unable to stand any more gawping, and sat down at the dressing table. 'Please take that moustache off, Albert, I can't bear the sight of it.'

'I'm not particularly keen,' he said, tugging at it and setting his teeth. 'There, it's gone.'

I set to work removing the eyebrows, and caught him watching me. 'Please don't look,' I said. I felt as if I were taking a layer of skin off with them.

'What is it?' he said, quietly.

I met his eyes. 'I'll tell you in a minute,' I said. 'I want to be clean first.'

'We can go and see Jemima and the baby tomorrow.' Albert put a hand on my shoulder.

'It isn't that.' I wiped the rest of my disguise away, and went to the bathroom to wash.

'That's much better,' said Albert. 'You look almost like yourself again.' He looked at me quizzically. 'But not quite.'

'I have something to tell you,' I said, sitting on the bed and patting the space beside me.

Albert raised his eyebrows. 'More news?' he asked, joining me.

'I'm not absolutely sure, but . . . you remember you said I looked green earlier?'

He nodded.

'I felt a bit sick. It's happened a few times in the last week. Particularly in the mornings. At first I thought it was an illness, but then I haven't — you know, the thing that happens every month. And when I read the telegram, I realised…'

'Oh my — so you're — we're —'

'I think so, yes. I mean,' I looked up at him. 'I might be mistaken, or it might not take, or —'

'Never mind might.' Albert's eyes shone. 'Never mind all that.' He put his arms around me and held me close. 'What a — what an *adventure!*'

CHAPTER 25
Katherine

Mr and Mrs King treated me as a second daughter from the moment I married James, albeit with only vague attempts at imposing the restraint on me that they had on Evangeline. They probably thought there was little chance I'd comply, given the exaggerations James had put on my adventures, but I was happy to call them Mama and Papa rather than be formal. It was impossible to think that I'd known the family for just four months. Hazelgrove already seemed like a second home, and when James suggested that Connie, Margaret and I stay for a week in July to get away from London I agreed, even though I'd be apart from him. It had been an exhausting four months.

'Are you quite comfortable, Connie?' said Mama. 'You look a little flushed, but then it is rather warm.' Mama was wearing an up-to-date dress in a soft mauve, having realised that she could no longer exactly recall whom it was she was mourning. 'I don't know where Baxter has gone. I'll go and see if she can bring more ginger biscuits. You do seem fond of them and they might help.' She peered at me in case I might be desperate for ginger biscuits too, then bustled into the house, leaving me and Connie on the shady terrace.

'I think she's guessed,' said Connie. She sat back in her chair, ran a hand over her stomach and looked up at Hazelgrove.

'Can you feel anything?' I asked. Connie's face still held a secret inner gaze. I wondered what it would be like to know a little being was forming inside, another whole person. I was almost jealous of her. Almost.

'Not through all these clothes,' she confessed, and poured us both more tea. 'But when I'm, you know, undressed, it feels different, there's a bump.' She blushed as if I would be shocked at the knowledge she wasn't always under four layers of clothes. The flush on her face was replaced by a sudden look of grey desperation.

'Still feeling sick?'

'Yes. I sometimes think it will never go away. Maria said it's usually finished by now. I didn't like to ask Jemima, and I haven't told Mother yet.'

'Why not?'

'Would you?'

I shrugged. It was hard to say. I would have told my own mother and I would probably tell Mama, once I had braced myself for being fussed over. Connie's mother was a different kettle of fish, although she was a doting if interfering grandmother to Jemima's little Arthur. At the moment, though, I was hoping not to have anything to tell for some time. I wanted James all to myself and that was hard enough to achieve anyway. I still yearned for the cottage on the cliffs.

As if reading my thoughts, Connie spoke. 'Of course, Margaret will be going away in a few months. Now that Mina is living with your aunt Alice, you and James will be positively rattling round. Unless you find you're expecting too…'

'Mmm,' I said. 'It seems rather a palaver. Maybe we won't bother. Separate bedrooms should do the trick.'

Connie blushed again, then grinned. 'I can't see you two managing that.' She sighed. 'But you're right, it is a palaver. I never knew how much equipment a baby needs until I saw everything Jemima has. And I am terrified of the thought of hiring a nursemaid.'

'Yes, but Jemima probably has everything you could possibly have, and more besides.' I looked at Connie sidelong. 'It will be terribly expensive if you go all out.'

Connie seemed to be considering how to respond. I felt terrible. What if they were in financial trouble, and I had touched a nerve? 'I'm sorry, Connie, that's your business, not mine.'

'No, it's quite all right.' She touched her stomach. 'I would have told you before, Katherine, but it wasn't my story to tell; it was Albert's. Now that everyone's beginning to find out, though…'

It was worse than I had thought. I'd always wondered how they managed to live so well on Albert's income.

He was the youngest son after all, even if he was a Lamont. 'Oh, Connie, I'm so sorry…'

She looked at me in complete astonishment. 'I beg your pardon?'

'There must be something you can do. Could you ask Uncle Maurice for a loan? Or your father?'

Connie stared at me, then began to laugh. I was beginning to worry about her. First down, then up. I hadn't realised how much pregnancy could affect a person. 'We're not going bankrupt!' she managed to choke out.

'Oh. Um, good.' I waited for her laughter to subside but there seemed little chance of that. 'So . . . what are people finding out?'

Connie calmed down enough to speak. 'That Albert's — ah — a bit wealthier than they thought. Investments.' She wiped her eyes with her handkerchief. 'It came out when his father questioned his management of the family money.'

Was I dreaming? 'Albert . . . manages the Lamont money?'

Connie nodded. 'He has done for a few years, privately. His father took back control for a month or two recently, before realising that actually it was much less bother to have Albert do it. But Albert told Moss, and then Moss told the other Lamonts, and now he deals with their personal settlements, too.'

It was like hearing that Margaret was secretly a professor of linguistics. 'So all those times when I've asked him for a ten-shilling loan, or felt bad that he paid for lunch, I needn't have done?'

Connie grinned. 'No.'

'And you won't have to move in with me and James?'

'No, and I'm sure you're very glad. In fact, we're looking for somewhere bigger. After all,' she smoothed her stomach, 'hopefully there will be more than one.'

Mama came bustling back with Baxter in tow, bearing fresh hot water and more ginger biscuits.

'Those naughty girls have been tormenting the ducks, but they're coming now,' she said. It took me a while to realise she meant Margaret and Evangeline. If Dr Farquhar had managed to persuade Papa that Evangeline was well enough to rejoin the outside world, Margaret's bounce and chatter had given them no space to argue. Margaret managed to mix fashion trends, society news and scientific ideas she obtained despite school rather than because of it into confusing but entertaining monologues. I had to kick her when she started on women's suffrage. Papa was a long way from realising that a woman was not a delicate flower who needed more care than an orchid.

The two of them came round the corner of the house and flopped into their chairs. Margaret was wearing her knickerbockers as she'd been cycling the grounds. Mama bit her lip.

'Don't worry, Mrs King,' said Margaret, 'I always change for dinner. I have one evening dress you haven't seen which I've kept for our last night here. It's been so lovely. Are you really sure I can come and visit when I'm at Somerville? Ooh, these biscuits look yummy. I'm ravenous. Do you think I should go to Somerville, Kitty? Only I was wondering about medicine. I had lots of lovely talks with Dr F about neurology. I could go to Edinburgh instead. What do you think? Would it be very cold? Perhaps I could study science at Somerville first. I can't wait to go. I think the other girls will be such fun. I don't think it's as stuffy as the others and besides, I've heard there are lots of political —'

I kicked her. 'Edinburgh's out of the question at the moment. Maybe in the future. You should be glad Uncle Maurice is helping.' I felt my face grow warm as I realised it was actually Albert who was helping. 'And you shouldn't have pestered Dr Farquhar so much that evening he came to dinner, before Mina moved out. No-one else could get a word in. And you put everyone off their food.'

'Dissection is interesting.'

'Not when you're eating mutton.'

Connie was looking green again. Mama snatched the plate of biscuits from Margaret and handed them over. 'Perhaps I should ask Cook to make some ginger tea?'

Connie shook her head.

'Are you going back to work for Dr F, now he's returned from his tour?' asked Margaret, helping herself to a scone. 'You ought to give up the Department. I can't believe the civil service has anything else exciting to offer. You'll just be typing for boring men who can't spell.'

'Oh, but Katherine doesn't need to work,' said Mama. 'James earns quite enough for both of them.

And if London is ever too much, they can live here. It is his home, and all this,' she waved a hand at the grounds, 'will be his one day.'

'Not for a long time, I hope,' I said, smiling and touching her hand. There was a little hint most days. I felt pulled in so many directions. Lovely Hazelgrove with its servants and grounds, our home in London with the noise and bustle and Ada, the cottage on the cliffs with... The last was unrealistic, like a lovely dream. It would never be the same if we went again. But James loved his job and I...

'Kitty doesn't just work for the money,' said Margaret.

How little she knew. Father had been missing for five years and in most of that time the only thing that had kept the tripe and mutton on the table had been me typing for boring men who couldn't spell. And yet... I glanced at Connie. Of all the people I could have met. If I hadn't, would I still be in that typing room, bored, irritated, miserable? Probably. How I yearned then to be back at home with no more to do than a little light dusting and ordering cutlets and beef steak, rehiring two more maids to help, drifting in my fashionable clothes from library to lecture to concert to church.

Was that what I wanted to do? Of course, if I was up to my ears in children it might be different. A feeling of despair washed over me. I didn't want them yet. Not yet. I just wanted James, and not to be bored.

'I'm sure she's very glad all her adventures are done with,' said Mama. 'And I'm sure you are too, Connie, especially at the moment. I expect you're both looking forward to just being ladies again.'

'Mmm,' said Connie. She caught my eye and I realised she felt the same as me. She didn't want to be bored.

***

We arrived back at Connie's house the following afternoon. It was still sunny but in London it was stuffy, the air smoggy, the light dimmed by smoke. Connie invited us in to freshen up and take tea before heading home. I was relieved. I wanted to go home, and I didn't. James wouldn't be there, and I hadn't yet handed in my notice to Mr Maynard, even though the work I was now doing for him was not particularly interesting. I felt at a crossroads.

I had suggested to Mina that she take my old role with Dr Farquhar. I wasn't surprised when she said yes. She was interested in the work, but Dr Farquhar, I suspected, was interested in her.

Connie had just opened her mouth to say something when a raucous ringing made us both scream.

'Whatever —'

'It's the telephone, madam,' said Nancy. 'The master had it installed when you were away. He thought it would surprise you.'

'Well it has. Hadn't someone better do whatever you do to stop it making that awful racket?'

The footman walked into the room. 'It's a call for Mrs King, ma'am. Could you follow me, please?'

'For me?'

I had no idea how to use a telephone but the footman gave me what he said was the receiver. 'You listen here, and speak here,' he said, pointing.

'Hullo!' I shouted into it.

'You needn't yell.' It was James, or at least I thought it was. 'This is important. Can you go home? I'll meet you there.' My heart jumped, and then I remembered that when I got home I would have Margaret with me. It wouldn't be quite the same.

'Are you there now? Have we got a telephone too?'

'Don't be silly. I'm waiting to see how much it costs Albert first. I've got other things to spend money on.'

'If I keep working —'

'Katherine, not now. Please, go home. I'll be there as soon as I can. It's important. Goodbye.'

I gave the receiver to the footman and felt annoyed. No 'I love you, I missed you'. Who did he think he was ordering about? But that wasn't his style. What was wrong? Had something happened to Ada? To Aunt Alice?

I explained to Connie and she summoned Tredwell back from the mews. Half an hour later, Margaret and I were at home.

'What's wrong?' I asked Ada as soon as we were in the hall. Everything looked the same as usual.

'Nothing Miss, Madam, Miss Kitty,' she said. 'Well, Elsie next door has run off with the butcher's boy. I knew there was shenanigans but —'

'Is Aunt Alice all right?'

'Yes, as far as I know. She came and brought flowers

earlier, said Mr James wouldn't think of making up vases for you.'

'No, he wouldn't.'

We put our bags down, took off our hats, and hung our coats on the rack.

'Could you bring us some tea please, Ada,' I said. 'You can tell me about Elsie later.'

Margaret and I stood in the hall feeling baffled. 'What was the rush?' said Margaret.

I didn't know what to say. A bang at the door made us both jump. I heard Ada curse in the kitchen.

'Don't worry,' I called, 'I'll answer it.'

On the doorstep stood Father. It took me a moment to recognise him. He had become an old man. His skin was sunburnt and peeling, his old-fashioned whiskers white. He was thin and his clothes hung off him. They had been very good clothes once and were clean, but tired and worn. As was he. At the bottom of the steps, a cabbie was unloading bag after bag.

We stood frozen, looking at each other. Father took me in from head to toe, as I was taking him in.

'Mathilda?' he said, then shook his head. 'Foolish, foolish. But surely you can't be Kitty. You were barely more than a child.'

'Father!' I flung my arms round him.

Margaret stepped out of the shadows of the hall and hesitated.

'Meg? But you were a little girl!' He put his other arm out.

'I was thirteen, Father,' said Margaret. 'Kitty was

twenty-two.' After a second she stepped into his embrace.

A rattle below us made me peer round Father's arm. I'd forgotten how tall he was. James had arrived. He took the steps two at a time. I stepped out of Father's embrace and into his.

'Unhand my daughter, sir,' said Father.

'Father, this is my husband.'

'Husband?' Father's mouth dropped open.

'We have a lot to tell you,' I said. 'You've been away a long time.'

'Nonsense.' Father shook his head, looking round the hall and noting his ancient raincoat with a smile. 'I've been gone hardly any time at all. Where are Annie and Clara?'

'Dismissed, Father. But Ada's still here.'

'Dismissed? Never mind, you must listen — Ah, Ada! You at least have not changed. I have brought you saffron from Byzantium. I have brought you dates from the Levantine. I have brought you —'

'Very nice, sir,' said Ada, as if he'd been out for half an hour. 'I'll get more cups.'

Father marched into the drawing room arm in arm with Margaret.

James held me back. 'I'm sorry,' he said. 'I had wind of it from someone at the paper. Your father wired the *Chronicle* from France to offer an interview, and gave a date when he'd be landing but not a time. I've had someone on watch at the port all day, since I couldn't be there myself. I didn't want to get your hopes up until I knew it was true.'

I could hear Father regaling Margaret. I needed to be there with her; she had looked completely lost.

'We have so much to talk about,' I said. 'This changes everything.'

'I know,' said James. 'I don't know what to say. I'm so happy for you and Margaret but…'

'But?'

'But I wonder if you will want to move away with me now.'

'Move away?'

'I was thinking of renting a house in Weymouth. I have an offer of a job at the local paper for six months. I thought we could have a place of our own, just the two of us and Ada, for a little while. But now…'

But now…

'Come along in, come along in,' called Father from the drawing-room doorway. 'I have to tell you what I've been up to. I never found the black tulips, although I don't suppose you knew I was looking. But I nearly found Noah's Ark. It's been a wonderful time. You must listen. I expect life has been very dull without me. Although perhaps you have had your own little adventure keeping house while I was away.'

'Telegram for Mrs King!' The front door was still open. I took the wire from the lad and opened it.

Please report office as soon as possible STOP I have a proposition STOP It does not involve typing STOP Even married women may apply even expectant women STOP Expect to see you both at nine tomorrow

241

Maynard.

'Who's Mrs King?' demanded Father.

'I am,' I said. 'And I haven't stopped having adventures yet.'

Acknowledgements

Our first thanks go to our beta readers — Ruth Cunliffe, Christine Downes, Stephen Lenhardt, and Val Portelli — and our excellent proofreader (and now expert on a few things he hadn't bargained for!), John Croall. Sending positive vibes and wafting goodwill (but not cats) your way! Any remaining errors are the responsibility of the authors.

In the course of writing this book (and also afterwards!) we came across all sorts of resources about the Victorian interest in matters supernatural. Here are a few of them:

'The Victorian Supernatural' by Roger Luckhurst: https://www.bl.uk/romantics-and-victorians/articles/the-victorian-supernatural

'How to Have a Seance: Tricks of the Fraudulent Mediums' by Troy Taylor:
http://www.prairieghosts.com/seance2.html

'19th Century Fortune-Telling: From the Drawing Room to the Court Room' by Mimi Matthews: https://

www.mimimatthews.com/2016/01/11/19th-century-fortune-telling-from-the-drawing-room-to-the-court-room/

If you would like to watch an example of cold reading in action, here is a YouTube video of Derren Brown demonstrating it very convincingly:
https://www.youtube.com/watch?v=13YaVfpjGL4

And finally, thanks to you, the reader, for getting this far! We hope you've enjoyed Katherine and Connie's exploration of things that go bump in the night, and if you could leave a short review of the book on Amazon or Goodreads that would be really helpful. As independent authors, reviews are one of the things which help readers find our work. Even a short review (or a star rating) is very much appreciated.

Font and Image Credits

Fonts:

Main cover font: Birmingham Titling by Paul Lloyd (freeware):
https://www.fontzillion.com/fonts/paul-lloyd/birmingham

Classic font: Libre Baskerville Italic by Impallari Type (http://www.impallari.com): https://www.fontsquirrel.com/fonts/libre-baskerville License — SIL Open Font License v.1.10: http://scripts.sil.org/OFL

Vector graphics:

Typewriter (recoloured and skewed): Typewriter Isolated Nostalgic by Gellinger: https://pixabay.com/en/typewriter-isolated-nostalgic-old-1138293/

Crystal ball stand (cropped, resized and recoloured): Snow Ball by Pixaline: https://pixabay.com/en/snow-ball-snow-white-december-1148834/

Teapot vignette: Vintage Teapot by Kaz: https://pixabay.com/en/vintage-teapot-coffeepot-coffee-pot-3115647/

Gloves vignette (cropped and recoloured): Wedding Gloves in the Metropolitan Museum of Art: https://www.metmuseum.org/art/collection/search/156934

All images used are listed as public domain (CC0) at source.

Cover created using GIMP image editor: www.gimp.org.

About Paula Harmon

At her first job interview, Paula Harmon answered the question 'where do you see yourself in 10 years' with 'writing', as opposed to 'progressing in your company.' She didn't get that job. She tried teaching and realised the one thing the world did not need was another bad teacher. Somehow or other she subsequently ended up as a civil servant and if you need to know a form number, she is your woman.

Her short stories include dragons, angst ridden teenagers, portals and civil servants (though not all in the same story — yet). Perhaps all the life experience was worth it in the end.

Paula is a Chichester University English graduate. She is married with two children and lives in Dorset. She is currently working on a thriller, a humorous murder mystery and something set in an alternative universe. She's wondering where the housework fairies are, because the house is a mess and she can't think why.

Website: www.paulaharmondownes.wordpress.com

Amazon author page: http://viewAuthor.at/ PHAuthorpage
Goodreads: https://goodreads.com/paula_harmon
Twitter: https://twitter.com/PaulaHarmon789

Books by Paula Harmon

Murder Britannica
When Lucretia's plan to become very rich is interrupted by a series of unexpected deaths, local wise-woman Tryssa starts to ask questions.

The Cluttering Discombobulator
Can everything be fixed with duct tape? Dad thinks so. The story of one man's battle against common sense and the family caught up in the chaos around him.

Kindling
Is everything quite how it seems? Secrets and mysteries, strangers and friends. Stories as varied and changing as British skies.

The Advent Calendar
Christmas as it really is, not the way the hype says it is (and sometimes how it might be) — stories for midwinter.

Weird and Peculiar Tales (with Val Portelli)
Short stories from this world and beyond.

About Liz Hedgecock

Liz Hedgecock grew up in London, England, did an English degree, and then took forever to start writing. After several years working in the National Health Service, some short stories crept into the world. A few even won prizes. Then the stories started to grow longer . . .

Now Liz travels between the nineteenth and twenty-first centuries, murdering people. To be fair, she does usually clean up after herself.

Liz's reimaginings of Sherlock Holmes, her Pippa Parker cozy mystery series, and *Bitesize*, a collection of flash fiction, are available in ebook and paperback.

Liz lives in Cheshire with her husband and two sons, and when she's not writing or child-wrangling you can usually find her reading, messing about on Twitter, or cooing over stuff in museums and art galleries. That's her story, anyway, and she's sticking to it.

Website/blog: http://lizhedgecock.wordpress.com
Facebook: http://www.facebook.com/

lizhedgecockwrites
Twitter: http://twitter.com/lizhedgecock
Goodreads: https://www.goodreads.com/lizhedgecock

Books by Liz Hedgecock

Short stories
*The Secret Notebook of Sherlock Holmes
Bitesize*

Halloween Sherlock series (novelettes)
*The Case of the Snow-White Lady
Sherlock Holmes and the Deathly Fog
The Case of the Curious Cabinet*

Sherlock & Jack series (novellas)
*A Jar Of Thursday
Something Blue
A Phoenix Rises* (winter 2018)

Mrs Hudson & Sherlock Holmes series (novels)
*A House Of Mirrors
In Sherlock's Shadow* (autumn 2018)

Pippa Parker Mysteries (novels)
*Murder At The Playgroup
Murder In The Choir
A Fete Worse Than Death
Murder In The Meadow* (2018)

Caster & Fleet Mysteries
The Case of the Black Tulips
The Case of the Runaway Client
The Case of the Deceased Clerk

Katherine and Connie will return in a new Caster & Fleet adventure:
Christmas 2018

Printed in Poland
by Amazon Fulfillment
Poland Sp. z o.o., Wrocław